HEARTACHE

HEARTACHE

A BOOK OF LOVE STORIES

Edited by MIRIAM HODGSON

Teens · Mandarin

First published in Great Britain 1990
by Methuen Children's Books
Published 1991 by Teens · Mandarin
an imprint of Mandarin Paperbacks
Michelin House, 81 Fulham Road, London SW3 6RB

Mandarin is an imprint of the Octopus Publishing Group

'The Dalgleish Women and the Game of Love' © Annie Dalton, 1990
'Crack Down' © Ian Strachan, 1990
'Sea Changes' © Jenny Koralek, 1990
'The Key' © Geraldine Kaye, 1990
'Cal' © Jean Ure, 1990
'Icebreaker' © Pete Johnson, 1990
'The Roseline Tapes' © Adèle Geras, 1990
'The Girl Who Loved the Sun' © Diana Wynne Jones, 1990
This volume © Methuen Children's Books, 1990

ISBN 0 7497 0655 4

A CIP catalogue record for this title
is available from the British Library

Printed in Great Britain
by Cox & Wyman Ltd, Reading, Berkshire

CONTENTS

'It's only the happy who are hard…
I think perhaps it is better for the
world if one has a broken heart.'

Helen Waddell, *Peter Abelard*

Foreword

Does love still hurt? In inviting writers to contribute to this collection I was occasionally asked whether writers today can still write about heartache. Did writers of a century ago have a monopoly? Has the sexual revolution, the liberation of women, killed the writer's gift of capturing heartache? I hope that readers of these specially commissioned stories will discover that the love story is as moving and passionate as ever in 1990, and that unhappy endings are still worth having.

Ian Strachan writes of the love that seems like betrayal, Pete Johnson of infatuation that has its funny side, while Diana Wynne Jones's story has the timelessness of myth and fairy tale, and shows how love gives one the power to change oneself. Adèle Geras reinterprets for our time one of the eternal stories of doomed love. Jean Ure writes about a love that neither war nor racial prejudice could dim. Jenny Koralek shows how something trivial and superficial can result in the loss of what might have been the great love. Geraldine Kaye captures the first love, the love one is not quite ready for, but likes the idea of. Annie Dalton writes about being confused, being afraid of love, and then realising that it can transform everything.

All the writers express the universality of falling in love, which is paradoxically always a unique experience to those who are in love, and always the strongest force in their lives.

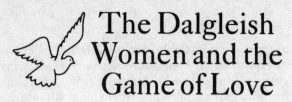

The Dalgleish Women and the Game of Love

Annie Dalton

I don't know how other people know they are going to fall in love, but the women in my family have a method that puts the tea-leaves to shame.

We lose my great great grandmother's camel bag.

I'd been told about the Dalgleish bag a hundred times of course, but I never took much interest. I suppose that was partly self-defence. There's a hopelessness that comes over the Dalgleish women when they talk about love that makes me grind my teeth, and entertain grim fantasies about taking the veil.

To hear them talk you could be forgiven for thinking that falling in love is the equivalent of being run over on a zebra crossing, except that the victims feel obliged to keep selling you the experience. 'Ah, but I knew I was living, then.'

I should explain that the Dalgleish family is peculiarly blighted in matters of love but that for some reason this just seems to make them even more enthusiastic about recommending it to others. Like people who carry on sending their children to sadistic schools where they themselves were utterly miserable.

Anyway, from a tender age, I decided to forsake men forever and be a person in my own right; a concert cellist, in fact. Because another drawback for the Dalgleishes, is our total inability to attract decent men into our lives and

1

keep them there. Probably this was always a genetic tendency but as far as I know the rot set in with Isobel, my great great grandmother, who dumped her Victorian bank clerk husband in Alexandria and went tearing off into the Sahara to have a fling with a beautiful sheik (the original donor of the camel bag), who had admired her red hair and her passionate playing of the pianoforte.

It was hushed up, of course, and then the bank clerk died and Isobel came back to England, sadder and wiser, it's to be hoped, to live out her days in Leamington Spa. Yes we are a dark-eyed bunch, and yes, I'm fairly sure we're not descended from the nice bank clerk, which is a shame as he might have had a restraining influence on the family chromosomes. As it is, the family history, after he departed it, reads like an Irish ballad, with weeping women and babes in arms being betrayed and abandoned all over the place by a shambling assortment of adventurers, poets and ne'er do wells.

Which brings me to Kate, my own mother (herself a rash product of the Second World War and an affectionate G.I.), who dashed off to San Francisco to discover her roots, fell in love with a rock musician called Arnold, married him and was deserted by him a couple of years later.

I have a signed photograph of him from his flower power period. He looks dreadfully ordinary and unshaven to me and I can't see how Kate was taken in for one moment by the tin peace badges and ethnic headband stuff. But to hear her talk he was a charismatic combination of Gandalf, if not Gandhi, and Francis of Assisi. She swears that as they walked across the park one day, barefoot and stoned, no doubt, a wild bird flew to his hand. That's how magnetic he was.

To give you an idea of just how hopeless the Dalgleish women are, I wasn't even conceived while they were married but years later when he stopped over to see her *en route* to doing a concert in Germany. 'At least I had you. That way I got to keep a part of him forever,' Kate says. She doesn't say that she was glad to have me, in my own right. The musician wasn't a total bastard anyway as he sent the money for my cello when I needed it and after that he even took an occasional interest in me. The thing I can't forgive him is my name, which I haven't used since I was eight and which I'm certainly not going to tell you now or it would ruin the credibility of my narrative.

Anyway, one day, the rock musician sprang a surprise. Some years ago, he found a guru; not a hairy Sixties one but an Eighties one with a degree in economics, and since then Arnold's not only started to shave more often but he's become a sort of pop peace emissary for the United States. He flies about organising get-togethers for young people in order to 'break down barriers and impediments between nations' and that sort of thing. It sounded rather vague to me, and also risky. I've noticed that some people, myself included, become attached to their barriers and impediments and don't want them even dented, let alone broken down. But Kate was radiant. She's a pushover for all that fuzzy love-speak. Then Arnold actually invited me to go to one of his camps. Extraordinary! I was excited when I heard it was going to be on an island the guru had bought especially. But it turned out to be a Scottish island and out of season.

So that's how I came to be the new owner of the Dalgleish ancestral camel bag at last.

'I suppose you'd better have this, then,' said Kate the night before I left, finding me struggling with a darning needle and a fraying canvas satchel. Then, with a funny look in her eye, she shoved the squashy mahogany leather at me, and barking, 'And don't you *dare* lose it,' she bolted from the room.

I'd have liked it better if I could have been immune to the way she did it. As if she was initiating me into that sorrowing community of cantankerous dark-eyed Dalgleish women forever. But actually I was pleased. Shamefully pleased, dear reader. As if I was not, after all, one distinct self but a quarrelling ship of selves, some of whom had stowed away when I had my back turned and had their own secret views about our destination.

It's a lovely thing in itself, the bag; practical too. Large enough to keep all the necessary stuff in; and though it's plain and very simple, the leather is beautiful if you rub it up with saddle soap. It glows as if reflecting firelight, perhaps remembering Bedouin cooking fires and camels standing around, casting biblical shadows upon the sand.

I suppose Isobel hadn't bargained for the reality of life in the desert, any more than Kate bargained for real life with magnetic unshaven Arnold. I don't suppose she'd given a thought to his wives, eyeing her behind their veils, or to the sand blowing into her piano for days at a time, clogging up the keys. And the sheik off planning raids, playing Arabian Knights. She didn't think it would come down to giving piano lessons in Leamington Spa any more than Kate guessed she'd be churning out rainbow striped jumpers for mail order customers for twenty-five quid each.

I thought about the Dalgleish women a lot on the train to Edinburgh and all at once I felt tearfully grateful to them for getting me this far. As if I was the lovely prize for all they'd gone through. I wanted to sing, sitting by the window, watching the strange sky heavy and yellow with unfallen snow. I was the first contented Dalgleish woman; free and unwedded as a peach tree.

It was rough, going to the island. There were quite a few of us, all squashed together very internationally on the little fish-smelling ferry, but we didn't speak or even smile much, being more concerned with keeping our lunch where it belonged.

Once it occurred to me (unworthily) that perhaps we were all chance products of Arnold's love affairs in various continents, now brought together as part of his guru's cunning plan for world peace, and for some reason this made me want to laugh out loud. But the honest truth was, it had just hit me, as a lifetime cynic and loner, how much I hate group encounters of every kind. Only the unexpected splendour of Arnold's invitation had blinded me to what I was letting myself in for until it was too late.

By the time the welcome committee got to us, the sky was dark and chaotic with falling snow.

'I'm Inger and I'm your focaliser for your stay,' said someone vibrantly. 'The bus will take you to your shared cabins. The first session will begin after supper with a group attunement. We must make every moment work for us.' Then she said something Kate would have loved, about the planet's entire future depending on a successful outcome.

Apparently I looked as baffled as I felt because the girl beside me, who had prised the suitcase out of my numbed hands and was heaving it into the bus, said accusingly, 'You haven't read your information booklet, have you? I bet you didn't even choose to come. When I think what I went through to get myself selected and you just landed up here because you knew someone. I can see it in your face.'

'I just wish someone would tell me what the first session is a session *of*,' I hissed, staggering after her up the steps.

'The Game, you idiot. Don't you know *anything*?'

'Oh, but I hate games.' I resolved to skip them in favour of a hot bath and later a quiet corner, free from group attunement, where I could read my book.

'But The Game is why we're here,' she said. 'Playing it is the sole purpose of our presence on this island if not of our entire lives.'

Oh, Arnold, I thought. A week-long snakes and ladders convention with a bunch of snowbound international morons.

The bus bumbled up the track in the snowstorm until it reached a row of wooden cabins. I managed to get my suitcase down by myself this time and was just congratulating myself when someone tapped me on the shoulder – and held out the ancestral camel bag.

'I suspect this is yours?' he said with care.

'Yes,' I said. "Oh, thanks. Thank you."

But I was furious and worse; frightened. Because everything and everyone had gone blurred and strangely slowed-down. I'd refused to listen to Kate's stories about the Dalgleish camel bag and its unpleasant talent for recruiting future lovers, but to have it returned to me by *an enemy*. For I saw at once that that was what he was. I saw everything about him. His arrogant face. The cheap awfulness of his jacket and trousers and the uneven kitchen-scissors haircut.

It was all in a moment. No time at all. If you catch your sweater on a nail it unravels before you know it. And the humiliation I felt was like that dream where you turn up at

6

school naked. I don't mean he looked at me sexually. It was more as if he knew at once the things I hide, even from myself. Like the secret stowaways. I hated him for that.

'You say "thank you," but I think you prefer to say something very rude,' he commented. 'I think you are actually most difficult person, Dalgleish.'

Then as I stalked past towards my cabin, he reached out and lightly touched the Fairisle cap I'd jammed on all anyhow to stop myself getting earache on the ferry.

'But I love your so silly hat,' I heard him say quietly as I vanished through the door, my face on fire.

Of course in the end I wasn't allowed to miss The Game. Supper was nice, if healthily vegetarian. Then we were ushered into what they called the Great Hall, which was actually a honeycomb of hexagonal areas, where tables were set out with complicated brightly-coloured boards and jewel-like counters. The group attunement was very embarrassing, involving a lot of silent unproductive hand holding. Inger told us we were inwardly clarifying our goals but I had clarified mine already. I hoped only to escape as soon as possible without being too bored or making too big a fool of myself. At least I didn't have to hold hands with my enemy in the cheap suit. The thought made me ill. I knew his name by now. Tomas. He was from Eastern Europe. Arnold spread his net wide all right.

The Game itself I found baffling. I've never been good at games, but at least I could usually spot the rules when they were pointed out to me. But with The Game the most important rules were hidden so that, for the obscurest reasons, you could be sent hurtling back to the beginning of the board time after time, to begin all over again. I was sweating with exhaustion by bedtime and I'd only moved a half square. I hadn't even begun the proper opening moves.

Then, as I went back to the cabins in the snow, someone was singing. It gave me a funny ache in my throat to hear our song in this lonely place.

> *'A woman is a branching tree*
> *and man's a clinging vine.*
> *And from her branches carelessly*
> *he'll take what he can find.'*

Kate and I sang it when I was little, driving bravely off to unsuitable holiday cottages in her Morris Minor. '*Let No Man Steal your Thyme*' it's called. She sang that and the one about love growing colder once it's older. Those were the real rules of the game, the unchangeable cosmic ones, I thought.

And I wished with all my heart I was home, practising the cello, washing my hair, quarrelling boringly with Kate. Anywhere but here.

Next day it took me until suppertime to move three squares. There was a party in the evening but I said I had a headache and went off to the Quiet Room in the hope they'd think I'd gone to meditate or something. It was a nice room with a fire and a lovely atmosphere that made me keep looking to see if there was incense or pot-pourri around somewhere. Now and then I could see blue flaring magically inside caves of coals. Then it was all ruined. *He* came in, with some others. I talked to his friends, though, not just to be polite but to show I thought he was poisonous. I was very animated and joked about Arnold and Kate and told the stories that always make people laugh. They laughed now. I noticed him once or twice looking at me as I smiled and talked and gestured, but on he sat and my face got hotter and hotter from the fire. And then I realised everyone else had drifted away. I got up in a rush then, but he said suddenly, 'Why do you tell such unhappy things like you are making so nice funny joke?'

'I don't know,' I said, hostile. 'But whatever it is, it's nothing to do with you.'

He stood up then and we glared at each other, eyeball to eyeball. 'You use clever labels to keep distance, Dalgleish,' he said. 'Distance from world. Make many very nice jokes. Always clever and very very quick so no one will ever get close and know you. You know what is truth? You are most difficult lonely person, Dalgleish.'

I was terrified when he said that. I had put on my bright borrowed colours and now they were draining away, leaving me no-coloured. No one. I was hurting more than if he had slapped me.

Then he said something worse. He said, 'You are not yet quite alive, Dalgleish. Like sleepwalker. But perhaps you could be woken – .'

And he leaned towards me, the space between us shrinking so easily I caught my breath, and his eyes were the same blue I had seen in the fire.

Almost I closed my eyes. But in time I saw he was laughing, his face shut as a knife, and I reared back so the kiss collided with air.

The room was too small. The island was too small. I couldn't get far enough away. I tore from the room and out of the building into the darkness, slipping, slithering on packed snow, hating him, oh, hating him. But even in my bunk bed with the covers over my head I could still hear the song.

> *'Beware, take care,*
> *keep your garden fair.*
> *Let no man steal your 'thyme'.*

Strangely, next day I did better at The Game. Maybe there was more to that attunement stuff than I'd thought because during it, this time, I'd decided to show Tomas I was a worthy enemy. Even so, it was still maddening to be role playing the Montagues and Capulets and have someone send you back five squares by tripping you up with a medieval bylaw or invoking the Romantic Predicament or whatever. But I was noticing more today and by lunchtime I had realised there were several different levels at which it was possible to play and because of that, to begin with, each player was effectively playing alone. I couldn't see quite how it worked after that. Then, as we were heading back to the honeycomb hall after lunch, I heard my name called, 'Dalgleish – I can't believe. You lose, once again, your valuable belonging.'

That damned bag. It had the most appalling taste. Throwing itself at feckless airmen and hairy rock singers. Probably its intelligence was wearing even thinner with age. I glared at the charmless individual in front of me, drawing a deep breath to tell him once and for all.

'No – ,' he checked me, 'don't thank again. I don't understand subtleties of your language. I may imagine you mean insult.'

I wanted to laugh then and he saw it because he said, in a different voice, 'Do you know what story I tell people when they ask about my country? I tell them about two-hat-cure for flu. Do you know what that is?'

I shook my head, distrustfully. He blew comically

upwards through the ragged fringe.

"You buy bottle of brandy and take with you to bed. Also you take hat. Hat you put down end of bed. Brandy you drink. When at last you see two hats you are cured.'

I laughed, genuinely at this but he said, 'Yes, all laugh at this story as everybody knows in my country we drink too much and I, of course, give sigh of relief that I have filled one more terrible silence. But you and I don't need to tell to each other such stories, Dalgleish.'

'Why not?' I said, becoming very still inside because once again everything had blurred and slowed down. You see, I was no longer so sure if he was my enemy. It seemed to me now that perhaps he was really my mirror. Looking at him, I saw myself reflected. And I was changing.

But all he said was, 'Hurry up, Dalgleish. If you go on improving at this Game you may make it into twentieth century by last day,' leaving me staring after him, clutching the ancestral camel bag and what I was thinking was that I didn't want to like him because falling in love for the women in my family is like suicide. They discard their lives the way someone loses a shoe in a train crash. Then after it's over they don't seem to realise, but limp around in a daze, like accident victims hopeful the shoe will be returned one day.

By teatime I had moved twelve squares and actually got to choose a Cosmic Helper. Someone had swiped Leonardo da Vinci and Emily Brontë so I thought I'd have Einstein, who seemed the right sort to help you out of a jam. Up until then I'd only incurred Debts and unleashed a few Furies. It was a funny thing; people came up and hugged me afterwards as if I'd made some kind of breakthrough. Actually, it occurred to me then that maybe not all of them were as awful as I'd thought at first.

That night the hall was thrown open to the real islanders for a ceilidh, and we could join in if we liked. Inger played something modest on an autoharp and other unlikely people did party pieces. To my astonishment Tomas came out, white and furious, and sat at the piano, cracking his knuckles. At last he launched into a Beethoven sonata and he was good. He was as good as anyone I ever heard. And when it was over he came to find me and I said, to prove myself a worthy enemy, 'It's a pity I haven't got my cello,' and he said, 'You still don't remember, do you? That competition in Bath, for young musicians?' And he had known me all along, had remembered me, whereas I am too nervous at competitions to see or hear anyone else. We talked quietly for a long time after this; real talking, and I'm ashamed to say some of the stowaways were beside themselves; opening out like hyacinths brought into a warm room.

Then someone said, 'Ssh, Morag's going to sing,' and a woman stood up from amongst the islanders and we hushed.

Morag was middle-aged, plain and flat-faced, with eyes like currants. Yet standing in front of us in her layers of shapeless clothes, she had the compelling authority of a great tree or an ancient rock. Finally she lifted her head and sang a desolate female lament, just as simply as a wolf would howl or the wind blow. Even those who grinned and squirmed to begin with were riveted. Even me. Probably not more than a dozen people in the room understood the words. Yet, as her song gathered beauty and power it expanded, catching us up, embracing us. For the space of a short human song we were all melded together as one.

Somehow my hand and Tomas's had come to rest side by side and slowly, although neither of us seemed to move, the distance between them decreased until I could feel his warmth as surely as if he touched me. But he did not clasp my hand and I kept the rules too. I kept my hand exactly where it was. It was only for the space of a song that we sat there hypnotised by the eloquent burning space between us, our faces betraying nothing. The faces of liars. Then Tomas looked at me and I knew he was waiting for me to speak this time; to make a claim on him. But I couldn't. And then he moved away, looking tired saying, 'I'll see you tomorrow then, Dalgleish. Let me know if you get any closer to the twentieth century.' And he left.

I couldn't sleep; turning everything over and over. Awarding myself points and taking them away. Stowaways ten. Captain of the ship nil. Archaic camel bag twenty-five. What was the use of caring for Tomas? He would only leave. At the end of the week he'd be gone. Safer to be solitary. Unwedded, like the peach tree.

> *'And every place*
> *where your thyme was waste*
> *will spread all over with rue —'*

Then I sat up in the darkness, electrified. What if the obsessive moves and counter moves, that the Dalgleish women had always imagined to be the game of love, were not The Game itself? What if they were only the first fumbling steps of something realer, wiser? Something we hadn't even begun to imagine yet? What if you didn't *fall* in love and lose yourself? What if you *walked* into love, of your own free choosing?

And then I knew why we were on the island and I

13

understood how much courage I would need to get through the rest of my life.

And later, days later by the water's edge, hugging him so hard I could feel him trembling, I still wanted to say, 'Don't, oh, don't make me want to live without you. Don't give me back the burden of finding my own way in the world. Be my home. Be my shelter, my other self. Be my happiness.'

But I couldn't. Because we'd brought the game into the twentieth century, and now the moves were new and unknown. And I kissed him again and my hat slipped and we had to rescue it before I climbed down alone into the boat.

'That silly hat,' he said. 'I love your silly hat, Dalgleish.'

I didn't look back. I wasn't going to shout farewells across a widening watery space. What I did was this. I unfastened the bag and I tipped out the contents, stuffing them in my suitcase, in my pockets, down the front of my jacket, anywhere. When the bag was empty I held it and silently thanked it. But from now on, I told it, I'm choosing my own beginnings and endings. And then I raised my hand and threw the bag over the rail, letting the water take it home. I would work out later what to tell my mother.

Crack Down
Ian Strachan

Abi hit my life like a bolt of lightning. I walked in through the school gates and there was this unbelievable girl wearing a combat jacket the size of a four-man tent. Her hair was jet-black, shoulder-length and dead straight. Her dark olive skin appeared to glow, her eyes were so dark they glistened like wet blackberries.

She stood astride a piece of knotted, tubular chrome sculpture they'd stuck on a lump of rock, to soften the image of our post-Alcatraz style buildings, singing, at the top of her voice, 'Don't Rain on my Parade'.

She was giving the last chorus some stick but got robbed of her round of applause by the bell which rang out off-key with her final note. We trickled away feeling embarrassed. New kids are supposed to slink in with their tails between their legs.

'Want to buy a girl a drink?'

I turned and was shattered to discover her phoney American talk was directed at me! Most girls didn't – bother to talk to me. They're into the Soccer 1st Team and Friday discos. 'You what?' I gulped.

'You look like a guy who knows his way around.' She talked out of the side of her mouth like Humphrey Bogart. 'Which way to City Hall?'

Heads turned as we walked to the Headmaster's office. Usually I'm a pane of glass but later I knew it wasn't only her they'd been looking at when everybody started cat-calling and making loud kissing noises on the backs of their hands.

I hated that! At least *mostly* I did but I also knew they'd

15

soon forget and I was surprised to discover I minded that more. Daft really, she'd got too much going for her to bother with a dimbo like me. The Soccer Team would eat her for breakfast.

I kept seeing her around. You couldn't miss someone who spends break barefoot, dancing in a big puddle, doing 'Singing in the Rain'. Though she was my age we weren't in the same set, so we didn't meet again until Friday. I'm in the bottom group for Art, I can't even draw a square box in perspective.

The second I walked in she started. 'Hi, big boy!'

The others groaned. Her novelty value had faded. I looked for a place at the back where I could read in peace.

She took the next desk. 'What's up? Cat got your tongue? My name's Abi. What's yours?'

'Mine's a Coke,' I said, trying to be witty.

'What does the "A" stand for Mr Coke?'

Before I could think of a snappy answer Barney, who looks like an owl and is rarely awake during the day, came in.

It was impossible to concentrate on my book. Sitting close to Abi was like being an iron filing in a magnetic field. Every time I turned towards her she was doing daft things like going cross-eyed, or lifting her eyebrows at the ends and blowing out her cheeks like a Buddha.

The biggest surprise was her drawing. Before Barney lapsed into deep self-hypnosis he pinned up a picture, for us to copy, of a woman in Elizabethan costume. Abi's drawing was fantastic, she'd caught the pose exactly, but the woman was timeless – she was stark naked.

'What you see is what you get!' Abi pouted and then, while I was still recovering, she whispered, 'Are you going to the disco tonight?'

I shook my head and buried it in my book though I couldn't help noticing that by the bell, when Barney fell off his perch to collect up the drawings, Abi had clothed the woman.

She collared me at the door. 'Why aren't you going to the disco?' She'd dropped the funny voice and fixed me with a look that felt like being caught in the full beam of a car's headlights.

I shrugged. 'I can't dance.'

'I'll teach you,' she countered flatly. 'I *want* you to take me.'

'Oh, come on! There must be hundreds of guys queuing up.'

She looked under each arm and behind the radiator. 'I can't see them.'

Then I twigged! She'd overplayed her hand – frightened them all off. The soccer team were stars who chose girls to bathe in their glory. Stars don't appreciate being outshone, much less eclipsed. Either that or she needed me as a foil, like flash girls choose plain ones to lessen the risk of competition.

'Mr A. Coke, I want *you* to take me,' she insisted.

'My name isn't A. Coke.'

'I know that! You're Pete Rowley, you're my age. You live near me in Vale Avenue. Your interests include collecting fossils and stamps but you're determined to take up hang-gliding and, when you leave school, become a secret agent.'

I grinned. 'How did you know all that?'

'I made it up.'

'Only the last bits, the rest was true.'

She hid behind the Humphrey Bogart voice. 'I like to know who I'm doing business with, honey. Pick me up at seven. I live at 28 Beeston Drive, just off The Strip!'

She was walking away before I had a chance to refuse, then something flashed across my mind. 'I used to deliver papers there. That's the Taylors' and they don't have any kids.'

She winked. 'They sure as hell do now! The stork made them a special delivery!' She walked off swinging her hips like Tina Turner.

I nearly didn't go, I hate discos, but I kept noticing the clock and when it got to ten to seven I changed.

Even when my hand was on the bell I hesitated to press it, but the door swung open and there was Abi wearing a short, stunning green dress and Mr Taylor saying, 'Hello, Peter. Have a good time but don't be back late.'

'We won't, Dad, I promise,' Abi said.

'What's all this "Dad" stuff?' I asked as we set off.

She slipped an arm through mine. 'I'm an orphan,' she said, playing it for all it was worth. 'A piece of flotsam, washed up on the beach of life's injustice.' Seeing I was none the wiser she added, 'The Taylors are my foster parents. They're thinking of adopting me, if I'll have them! Come on, let's have fun.'

And that's what we did, have fun, and plenty of it, for the next six months, during which my life changed totally. It was like sitting on a rainbow eating chocolate ice-cream after living underground eating cold porridge sandwiches.

I was an only child and my parents weren't the kind who hugged and kissed but Abi was very physical, always stroking my arm, or running her fingers through my hair, giving me a whole set of new sensations. I felt born again, as if Abi had stripped off my protective layer leaving all my nerve endings exposed.

I also found there was another side to her. She still did crazy things, like the time she waved goodbye from a coach full of American tourists and spent two days hitching back from Edinburgh, but sometimes she liked to do very ordinary things, like feed the ducks in the park. She was always so determined each duck got its fair share. I loved the peace of the quiet times and it was during those that I began to find out more about her and to understand her better.

Once we were climbing the hill outside the town when Abi told me she was two weeks old when her mother dumped her on her Gran.

'The only thing my Mum gave me was my name – Abigail.' Abi pulled a face. 'But I soon changed that.'

Gran was too old to know how to cope and she ignored her. Which was when Abi started to do outrageous things, simply to get Gran to notice her.

'I was about four. We'd gone shopping, which I hated because I was supposed to trail round without touching. Well, that day I found my own amusement. I ripped the labels off fifty food tins. I know it was fifty because Gran counted them when I gave her them outside.'

We paused for breath. 'What happened to your Gran?'

'She died when I was seven.' Abi gazed out over the town below us. 'I'd no other relatives so I was put in a Home. "Abigail Simpson, This is Your Life!" '

'You've lived in a Home ever since?'

'Yes, and with about ten sets of foster parents.'

'Why didn't you stop with them?'

'Because they couldn't take the pace! People foster kids for all kinds of reasons. Some use you to fill gaps in their own lives, like completing a set of stamps; some do it for the money they get paid. Pete, you think *I'm* weird, you haven't lived! I've stayed in houses that reeked of boiled cabbage, where husbands and wives never, I mean *never*, spoke to each other.' Abi fell silent as she thought back over her life. 'What had I got to lose? I started with nothing, I wanted something better, not something worse. When things got boring, or didn't work out I pulled some spectacular stunt and bingo – I was back in the home again.'

Abi irritably brushed the hair out of her eyes. 'Trouble is, I'm running out of time. If I don't get adopted soon I never will, I'm heading for the last round up, kid!'

'The Taylors? Surely they're OK?'

Abi shrugged. 'I guess – bit dull and respectable, but they'll do, I suppose.' Abi put her arms round her shoulders and hugged herself tight as if to show the love she'd wanted and missed all her life.

I stroked the back of her neck as we kissed but, even with my arms round her, a cold unease crept up my back at the thought of losing Abi if she left the Taylors. Abi had become the core of my life. Living without her would be like living without arms or legs. I could never go back to being the self-contained person I once was.

Abi snapped me out of it. 'Come on, Superman! Let's fly over Gotham City and see how the citizens are making out.' She grabbed my hand.

'I can't fly.' I still resisted her fantasies.

'Together we can!'

Maybe it was that bit of the old me, the bit that was happy to watch Abi doing amazing things but reluctant to join in, that drove a wedge between us. Or maybe what satisfied me wasn't exciting enough for Abi who was constantly seeking new sensations. Maybe she'd looked too hard for too long and didn't know what she wanted.

Whatever it was, things suddenly changed for no particular reason and we no longer spent every spare minute together.

'I'm tired, I think I'll stay in this evening,' she said when I suggested going to the cinema.

Movies were meat and drink to Abi and I'd never known her refuse an offer but she wouldn't change her mind.

I was halfway through my homework when I realised I'd got some of Abi's books. Glad of any excuse to see her, I took them round.

Mr Taylor answered the door. 'Thanks for the books, Abi's out.' He noticed the astonished look on my face. 'To be honest I thought she was with you.'

'She said she was staying in because she was so tired.'

Mr Taylor nodded. 'I thought so too. In fact I wanted a word about keeping Abigail out so late.'

'You said ten o'clock weekdays and midnight Fridays and Saturdays.'

'I did and if you'd stuck to that it would have been all right but three and four in the morning isn't good enough!'

I was stunned but I didn't give her away. I didn't say anything to Abi either, but next time we went out and parted at the end of her road I waited in the shadows for her bedroom light to go on. Seconds later she passed me heading back for town. I followed her to a disco, a real dive, with a reputation for drugs and underage drinking. It was two o'clock when she came out, leaning on a bunch of guys. They drove off together.

Feeling sick, I waited near her house until four in the morning. When the car pulled up Abi staggered out looking a wreck!

'Where've you been?' I asked, stepping out of the shadows.

She swayed round, forcing her eyes to focus. 'Pete! Dear old Pete! Where are you off to?'

'I'm waiting for you. Where've you been?'

'Having fun!' She staggered. Thinking she was drunk, I grabbed her but under the street lights her pupils looked the size of pennies and I knew she was on drugs.

I know now I should have done something straight away but I dared not tell the Taylors in case they packed her straight back to the Home!

We met less and less but every time Abi looked worse. Gone was the zany, attractive girl I'd fallen in love with. During the day, if she bothered to turn up for school, she was morose. Only under the influence of drugs was there the slightest sign of the old Abi.

'You should try Crack, Pete. It makes you feel fantastic.'

'Don't you realise you're frying your brains?'

'That's your trouble, Pete, you're scared to try new things. Come on, just once.'

I didn't try it then and I never have since. 'My brain may not be the best in the world,' I told her, 'but it's the only one I'm likely to get and I don't intend scrambling it for a quick sensation.'

Others weren't so reluctant. She persuaded several kids at school to buy some. No longer just a user but a pusher as well, a deadly combination. It doesn't take a genius to work out that a pusher who uses is likely to help themselves to the stock and end up owing their supplier a stack of money.

After a couple of months people started looking for Abi. A kid came up to me at school shaking all over, his nose and eyes streaming. 'Where's Abi? I've got to find her.'

I asked around. Nobody had seen her, then one girl said, 'You're not the only one who's asking. There were a couple of old guys hanging round the gate yesterday – something about money she owed them.'

The Taylors hadn't seen Abi either and, by the sound of it they didn't much want to, except to recover a valuable gilt carriage clock and a few other things which had disappeared with her.

It took me three days to find her. I was on the point of giving up when I took a short cut through an old terrace the council had bought but hadn't finished knocking down. I caught sight of a figure in the distance dodging into one of the buildings. Only a glimpse, but I recognised Abi immediately.

I followed but at the last minute stepped on a pane of glass which snapped like rifle shots. When I got inside she'd gone but I found an old blanket and some chocolate wrappers. Convinced this was the only place she had to hide I knew she'd be back. I bought some food at the off-licence and crept back to wait.

When it got to midnight and there was no sign of her I began to wonder if I'd frightened her off for good. Then I heard footsteps. I gave her a few seconds to settle before I snapped on my torch.

Abi was huddled, terrified, beneath the remains of the staircase shivering in her muddy combat jacket. Her face was grubby and tear-stained, her fingernails chewed down and her hair a greasy, tangled mass.

'It's only me,' I whispered. 'I've brought you some food.'

She snatched the bag out of my hand and rammed a pork pie into her face. Holding it there tight, the way a

23

monkey holds a fistful of food, she chewed through it. After that she gobbled up a cake and an apple without stopping.

Part of me was revolted, but there was another part that remembered how she once was, a beautiful, dancing moth who couldn't resist flames.

'I forgot to get a drink,' I apologised.

She kicked a baked bean tin towards me and pointed. In what was once the kitchen a lead pipe ran up the wall to a dripping tap.

Her mouth crammed with food, she gulped water. Some ran down her chin but she flinched when I tried to wipe it away.

'Does anyone else know I'm here?' Abi asked.

I shook my head. 'You can't stay though.'

Before she could answer she clutched her stomach and her knees jerked up to her chest with pain. Through clamped teeth she hissed, 'I ate too quickly.'

She cupped a hand to her mouth, retched and only just made it to the front door before she threw up; everything, non-stop. She came back wiping her mouth with the back of her hand. 'What a waste!'

I shrugged. 'I don't mind.'

'I do! I'm bloody starving. Find me some more food, anything.'

This wasn't my Abi. I wanted to walk away but when she flashed her brown eyes at me, despite the mess she looked, I knew I was still hooked and that I had to help.

My options were limited and either way I knew I was going to lose Abi. If I could find her it wouldn't be too long before others did. I could give her money to run away with but the guys looking for her specialised in contacts and they didn't like being made monkeys of. Sooner or later they'd catch up with her. The longer it took, the more they'd take it out on Abi. I had to put her beyond their reach and to do that I needed help. The Taylors were out of the picture, anyway they didn't need the hassle.

Which only left one awful frightening choice.

'You bastard!' Abi screamed at me, as the policewoman gripped her firmly. Then she suddenly seemed to switch back for a second to the old Abi. 'You're just no fun any more!' Then she tapped the police driver lightly on the shoulder. 'The Ritz, James, and step on it.'

I never saw her again, not close up.

She was done in the Juvenile Court for the theft of the clock but she was lucky and got probation on condition that she went into a residential addiction centre.

Several times I wrote to try and explain why I'd done what I had. I hoped that once she'd calmed down she might begin to believe it wasn't a betrayal but a clumsy attempt on my part to rescue her. I told her that none of what had happened changed the way I felt about her.

They weren't very good letters. They weren't the letters I wanted to write, they'd have been full of poetry and stuff. I couldn't even tell her what I was doing because I wasn't doing much.

She never wrote back – I don't know if she read mine.

I tried to see her.

The Centre was in this big old house. I stood at the top of some stone steps while an attendant went over to tell her I'd come, and I could see her sitting in the garden. She was thinner than I remembered. Her skin had lost its glow and her hair no longer shimmered in the afternoon sun.

She glanced across at me and I thought I saw a half-smile of recognition. Though there was none of the all-singing, all-dancing Abi, there was something about the way she tossed her hair back that made me think she hadn't forgotten what we'd been to each other but she sat back, looked away and shook her head.

Next time I went they said she'd transferred to another Centre but they wouldn't tell me where.

Everyone says I'll get over her. Maybe I will. Perhaps the pain of losing her will ease but not the longing, the aching gap she's left in my life.

Maybe she'd been searching too long. She was afraid to let things settle, had to keep stirring up the mud in the pool, because once they did then she'd have to commit herself and she'd been let down too badly in the past to trust any one person again.

That could be why she always backed off, like she did from me at the very moment we meant so much to each other.

Or else, though she never would have admitted it, she'd lived so long in institutions she felt safer there because they *were* impersonal and couldn't hurt her.

But she'd have to come out sooner or later – what then?

Kids at school said she brought it all on herself. They'd only seen her as a show off and didn't realise it was one big cry for help. They didn't know the Abi I'd held in my arms, crying when the sun set because she couldn't cup its dying, coppery rays in her hand.

I'll never know what the months we spent together meant to Abi but during them I felt whole. Now I feel like a twin constantly searching for my other half. Though sometimes I think, in saving Abi, it was me I lost.

Sea Changes
Jenny Koralek

I should have known. That very first day when Tom wasn't there. I should have known. It was an omen. From the start there was a jinx on us, a jinx on what was meant to be a wonderful holiday, the best ever.

Sarah came running up as soon as we drove into the campsite. Her sweet, round face filled the open car window like the moon.

'Tom Holt won't be here for another week,' she said. 'His mother's not well.'

All the excitement, all the dreams which had kept me in a happy, humming haze all the way down the motorway on the long journey from the north, all my feelings that being specially wanted I was being specially waited for, drained out of me. The little town of Wells suddenly looked dead, dull; the campsite of caravans and trailers like a prison compound under a sky I now saw was grey.

'Never mind,' Sarah was saying. 'There's some other nice boys here. You can come out with us if you like. Help the time to pass.' And she tilted her head towards a group of boys and girls hanging round the steps of her parents' trailer.

Sarah's family and mine have been coming to Wells for years. We go to the same school. We're in the same class. We make a good pair. She takes life as it comes. I don't. Most of the time we balance each other out, but just then I could have hit her. Did she seriously think spending time with her and that flirty gang she likes to go round with on holiday could take my mind off days wasted without Tom?

Tom's in our class too. Has been since we were all eleven. But we didn't notice each other till this Easter. From one day to the next Tom shone out for me and from the way he looked at me I knew I was shining out for him. How graceful he seemed in his rather fancy clothes. I liked the way he kept his shirt unbuttoned enough to show his jutting collar bone. I liked the feeling, whenever we had a chance to get close to each other, that at any moment our wrists might touch. I liked the way his mischievous eyebrows shot up in class when he thought something was funny. I liked him to catch my eye, mine alone. I started looking in every passing mirror. Did he like my hair, I wondered? My thick curly hair. Dad's always said it's got copper tints. I began to think I could see them too. And my eyes. Did he like my eyes? My hands? Was I altogether lovely enough for him?

He gave me answers the first time he kissed me. In the park after school, under a huge hawthorn tree. It was in May and hot. Was it only in May? It seems a hundred years ago. I remember his warmth, my warmth. His lips, my lips. Eyes closed and this new strong feeling flowing through us and between us.

'I want to be with you like this all the time,' Tom whispered. Or did I whisper it? Or did the words whisper themselves? I remember the spicy smell of the little tight white flowers just above us and knowing they were bound to open and summer was bound to come with its long days of light and freedom.

'I wish you could come to Wells,' I said.

'I'm working on it,' he said. And, thanks to Sarah badgering her soft-hearted mum who, it turned out, knew Tom's mum from work, Tom told me, after half-term, like a miracle, my wish had come true. So of course I'd been building up dreams ever since. That'll teach me. I know now nothing's certain. Nothing. Ever. But that day, all I knew was that Tom wasn't there.

I felt so bloody unhappy I got out of the car and walked straight to the far end of the site out on to the big beach. Of course Mum, Dad, and my little brother Jamie squawked and bellowed for me to come and help unpack, but I just walked on, out on to the great, long, wide, endless beach away from everyone. 'Leave me alone,' I yelled into the wind. 'Leave me alone.'

It sounds crazy, but I'd never been on that beach before. The one by the campsite had always seemed fine – loos and an ice-cream kiosk and a couple of shops. Not too far to run back if you'd forgotten your suntan lotion and a quick walk into Wells. But this beach seemed to go on forever. Of course it wasn't empty but it was so huge people looked like specks on it. I kicked off my shoes, rolled up my jeans and stomped along by the water where the sand was wet but firm enough to hold me. And I walked and walked, aching. What sort of days, what sort of evenings was I going to have without Tom? I must have walked for miles, raging and aching, because suddenly I realised I was the only person who'd come so far. Then I saw a figure in the distance. God, I thought, isn't there anywhere without people?

It was a boy, standing barefoot in the dunes, staring out to sea through a pair of binoculars. I often wonder now if he'd also had a look at me through them long before I got to him because, without letting go of them he said, 'Hi. There are seals out there. Do you want to have a look?'

He was wearing frayed jeans with holes in the knees and a T-shirt all unevenly stretched and stained with paint or something. He had tawny hair nearly as long as a

Sixties' hippy. When he let go of the binoculars I saw his brown, brown eyes.

'Thanks,' I said. I peered through the lenses but I couldn't see a thing.

'You'll need to focus them to suit you,' he said.

'Oh,' I said, feeling clueless. We didn't go in for nature stuff in my circle of family and friends.

'Shall I show you?' he asked.

'Okay,' I said.

I noticed his hands, too, while he fiddled with the black bits and showed me what to do. Slender, sensitive, strong. I remember wondering how I could find a complete stranger's hands and eyes so attractive if I was in love with Tom, but I did. He was saying, 'Any luck? Can you see them?' He sounded so much as if he really wanted me to see the seals and delight in them as he did, that suddenly I wanted to see them too. I struggled to get the focus right and there they were: far out to sea, smooth round heads, huge gentle eyes, bobbing and swimming like happy kids.

'Can you see the terns too?' said the boy. 'Look up a bit. See? See how they dive all of a sudden to get the fish?'

Yes, I saw them and the seals again and the other little birds strutting along the waterline. I lowered the glasses and took in the wide horizon stretching, curving out and out, that silver line where sky and sea meet and you don't know anymore where things begin or end. I felt part of something bigger than me and my sorrows, something which just gets on with life. There were the waves, coming and going. The water colour was changing as the sun began to break through the cloud. I heard the sea sounds. I saw the seals out there. I heard the birds with their sad, strident calls, wheeling and dipping. I remember thinking how magical it was that an unknown boy had shown me a new way of looking at the world. I remember smiling at the boy and him smiling at me.

'Makes you wonder, doesn't it?' he said.

'Wonder what?'

'Well…who set the ball rolling? And why? And what for? And how can we take care of the planet? It's all so beautiful and so intelligent…it can't all be for nothing…or can it?'

'Oh, don't,' I heard myself say. 'I know that shivery feeling…I get it when I look at the sky on a clear night…'

'Do you? Do you?' he said eagerly. 'You should come down here and see the stars over the sea…'

We looked at each other and it was like finding another traveller on a long journey you thought you were making all alone.

'I'm Jake,' the boy said. 'What's your name?'

'Franny,' I said.

'Franny,' said Jake. 'Franny.' Never had my name sounded so sweet.

'If you look through the binos,' he went on, 'you can see where I'm staying.'

I could see a small cluster of houses and a windmill by a landing-stage.

'Yes, in that wacky old windmill. My grandad lives there, only he's ill in hospital in Norwich, so Mum and I have come down from London to be near him till he's better.' He looked round.

'I love it here. Do you live here all the time?' he asked enviously.

'No,' I said. 'We're…I'm on holiday…in the caravan site…'

'Oh,' said Jake. 'I don't go into Wells much. It's too

crowded. You get sick of crowds if you live in London…'

'I've never been to London,' I said. 'It must be great – so much to do, so much to see.'

'Oh, I'd rather live here *any* day,' said Jake. 'There's room to breathe here…room to move without being hassled. Gives you a chance to…oh, I don't know…'

'Get nearer to your shivery questions?' I asked shyly.

'Yes!' said Jake. He smiled at me again. But I didn't know what else to say. Tom and I had never talked like this. Not about things that really matter.

'Well,' I said. 'I'd better be getting back.'

'Will you come this far again?' asked Jake. 'For a walk? Or we could take grandad's boat out to Seal Island?'

'Yes,' I heard myself say. 'I'd love to.'

'Why not?' I said on the way home. 'He's nice. I don't see why I shouldn't enjoy myself till Tom comes.'

That's how it began. We went to Seal Island and Jake taught me to row. When I felt his hands on mine it was different from touching Tom.

It was just as electric but I felt a gentleness I had not known before, a promise of trust and truth.

We didn't meet every day as I knew Mum, Dad and Sarah would get suspicious if I kept going off on my own. In fact, now I count it up we only met three times. Once to go to Seal Island where we saw no seals and twice at the dunes where we lay on our backs in the shifting sand, lazily letting it trickle through our fingers, gazing at the great sky. Although we lay close there was space between us for talking or not talking, telling or not telling our dreams, our secrets, our fears, our hopes, our likes, our dislikes and all the silly, sweet, little things. Space and time. Sooner or later I knew I'd end up resting my head in the soft place on his shoulder. I knew that whatever we did it would be right. It would be good.

After Seal Island I said to myself: 'Serve Tom right for not being here,' which wasn't fair. The first time at the dunes I thought: can you love two people at once? The next time I thought: I don't care, I don't care about anything except being here with Jake and I begged him to come to the dance in Wells on the last Saturday of my holidays.

'I'll think about it,' he said. I hoped he was teasing. When Sarah told me Tom was arriving the next day I had to tell her about Jake.

'Oh, God!' she said, 'Body *and* soul.' '*Serious!*' No wonder you're confused…'

'Shut up!' I snapped.

'Sorry,' she said. 'I'm jealous, that's all. But what are you going to say to Tom?'

'I don't know,' I groaned.

'You'll get it right at the time,' she said kindly.

Tom was tense when we met. If anything, more nervous than me. At first he stuck with the crowd, but at the end of the first day he came up to me and said, 'Franny, I don't know how to say this. Don't get me wrong. I really, really like you but… I don't know what happened. I'm sorry, but I don't seem to feel the same any more. Oh, God, I'm so confused…'

'It's okay,' I said. 'So am I.'

'Are you?' he sighed. 'Perhaps it just happens like that sometimes. But it was… it was… good, wasn't it?'

'Yes,' I said. 'Yes, it was. And Tom, I don't see why we can't still be friends.'

'Sure,' he said. 'Sure. Thanks, Franny. Thanks for understanding.'

'Let's go for a Coke,' I said, 'with Sarah and the gang.'

That night in bed I felt so relaxed, so free, so *happy*. 'Oh, Jake,' I whispered as I fell asleep. 'Please come to the dance. Please. Please.'

He did and it was awful. He was not the boy I had known on the beach. I couldn't see the Jake I knew shyly hidden by this awkward, spruced-up stranger who'd had a haircut and used gel or brilliantine to slick himself up; who was wearing dark trousers with red braces and a white shirt and a waistcoat, a striped silk waistcoat, and who tried so hard, too hard to be cool, to be like the other boys. I couldn't speak to him at all even though, when our hands touched briefly I felt his real nearness in spite of the clothes and the awful hair.

'Excuse me,' I said. 'I must go to the loo.'
When I came back he'd gone. Why didn't I go after him? Why didn't I take his hand and run down to the sea? We could have thrown off all our fancy clothes and plunged into the water and washed ourselves back to our true selves again. The gel out of his hair, the make-up off my face. After all I must have been a stranger, too, with my hair combed back and my short skirt and stilettos, my jingly bracelets and that strong perfume and lipstick Mum doesn't like. That's why I hurt. That's why I feel angry with him and with myself: all our silly ideas about wanting to impress and look where it got us.

Of course I went back all the way along the beach next morning early before we left. I ran all the way, all the way to the windmill. Even when I saw it was all shut up I kept on banging desperately till some old woman came out of her cottage.

'They've gone,' she said.
'What do you mean, gone?'
'The old man died,' she said. 'Dear old Jack Turner.

Died. In the ambulance on the way to London for emergency treatment. Of course they went with him. Must have been a shock. Funeral's tomorrow,' she droned on.

'Where?' I snapped.

'Somewhere in London. I don't know where. They didn't say and if they had it wouldn't mean anything to me. I've never been further than Norwich myself…'

'Shut up,' I was saying inside. 'Shut up. I'll find him. I'll find him.' He must be in the phone book. But I didn't even know his surname! I'd thought there'd be plenty of time for names and addresses. My Gran's always going on about how casual young people are, never introducing themselves properly. I cursed her for being right.

'Do you know what their surname was?' I asked the old woman.

'I don't,' she said. 'She was a married daughter. I just called her Annie and the boy…' She groped in her dusty old mind.

'Jake?' I said harshly.

'Yes, that's right, Jake. A nice lad, so natural, not afraid to be himself…'

That's what you think I thought bitterly, unfairly.

'…not like the boys round here…all dressed up and nowhere to go. No, I don't suppose they'll be back. Sell up to holiday makers most likely…'

I turned and ran to the dunes and flung myself down. I made a hollow for my body and curled up like a sick animal. The sand felt cold against my cheek. Jake, I groaned. Jake, Jake, Jake. Sarah's words came back to me, *body and soul, body and soul*. Jake and the seals. Jake and the birds. Jake and the sea and me. Only just found and now lost. Oh, Jake, come back. Come back. Ask me again who set the ball rolling and I'll look for the mindblowing answer with you.

Will I really never see you again? Can someone really disappear, in this piddling-sized country, in 1989?

God I hurt. God, I never knew I could feel this sad. How huge the beach. How huge the sea. And empty, empty, empty.

The Key

Geraldine Kaye

First day of term, 'Lord receive us with thy blessing,' up-ended trunks blocking the corridor, clothes laid out on beds waiting for matron to check, the slamming of drawers, the smell of disinfectant and noise from dawn to dusk. Holly completed her fourth walkabout of the school buildings and came back to the dormitory. Paul wasn't back yet. But at least Ruth had the next bed.

'Holidays okay?' Ruth said, still shining from her fortnight of pony trekking on Exmoor.

'Fantastic,' Holly said. How many times had she said it already? How could she say, '*Awful*, the most miserable weeks of my life.' It was against the rules. Nobody wanted to hear things like that.

'Where are all the hangers?' Ruth said flinging back the door of the shared wardrobe. 'Somebody's pinched them.'

'I'll go and get some more,' Holly said, glad of the excuse. On her fifth walkabout she found Sebastian sitting on the line of chairs outside the headmaster's study.

'Hi,' she said. 'Had a good holiday?'

'Naff,' he said screwing up his face expressively. 'Monaco is for pseuds. Utterly shonky, if you want to know.'

Of course, Sebastian made a thing of breaking rules. Mendip School was 'progressive', and there weren't that number of official rules. But the other sort of rules, the not-said, not-done things, they were infinite. Sebastian might have said more but Mr Radley came out of his study.

'Ah…Holly, isn't it?' Mr Radley said. He was a tall man, grey-haired, kindly and vague. 'Er…got over your little…er…mishap of last term, I hope?'

'Yes, thank you, Mr Radley,' Holly said going pink. Didn't anybody ever forget anything in this place.

'Good, good. GCSE this year, isn't it? Mr Page was telling me your photography is…er…promising. Keep it up, Polly…er…Holly. Ah, Sebastian, come along in.'

The study door closed behind them and suddenly Paul was coming down the corridor. Holly always saw him before he saw her. It was a sixth sense and it gave her time to get her expression right.

'Hi,' he said. She had the odd impression that he was walking on tiptoe. 'Had a good holiday?'

'Fantastic,' she said and now it was true. Seeing Paul, the special smile he gave her, the very best of his special smiles, cancelled out the weeks of waiting for a letter which never came; the fortnight on the Isle of Wight with her parents; the long dismal weeks with her aunt and uncle and cousin, Angie, at Hendon. All the holidays she had wished the days away, scolding herself for messing things up last term and getting everybody into trouble. How she longed to get back to school where she could at least see Paul every day. 'I took loads of photos,' she added.

'Did you get my postcard?' he asked lowering his voice, and then glancing at Mr Radley's study he whispered urgently, 'I've got to see you, Holly. It's important. Have you got the key?'

'I've still got *mine*,' Holly said clutching the front of her blouse protectively. She had worn it on a ribbon round her neck all the summer holidays. 'Do you want it?'

'Not here for God's sake,' Paul whispered as a group of noisy third years erupted into the corridor. 'Not now.'

'Where then?' she asked, and confusion made her reckless. 'Weston, Saturday afternoon? Same place, same time?'

'You're on,' Paul said dismissing her with a thumbs-up and sitting down in the chair where Sebastian had sat. Belinda was pushing her way through the third years.

'There you are,' she said to Paul and then her eyes, reddish-brown like beechnuts, turned to Holly.

'Good holidays?'

'Great,' said Holly walking away as Belinda sat down by Paul whispering, 'What's all this about?'

Two minutes later Holly threw herself on her bed.

'I saw Paul,' she said. She had to explain because she couldn't stop grinning like a Cheshire cat. 'And Sebastian and Belinda outside Mr Radley's study.'

'Expect he's trying to make up his mind about the new head of school,' Ruth said. 'Did you get the hangers?'

'What?' said Holly.

'Hangers, you dodo. You went to get some hangers, remember? I hope you're not going to be mooning around all this term too. Everybody knows it's Paul and Belinda.'

'Course not,' Holly said with the grin dying. 'Anyway he sent me a postcard from Spain.'

'Big deal,' Ruth said stomping off in search of hangers herself. Holly lay on her bed and wondered how she could get through the next four days.

On Saturday Ruth was going pot-holing with Mr Page, the PE teacher, and Holly took the early bus to Weston-Super-Mare. She cut lunch. She was far too excited to eat anyway. She carried the camera which her parents had given her for her fifteenth birthday and which she took everywhere. *Same place* was a seat near the pier; *same time* was three o'clock. The tide was out but coming in. She snapped the grey expanse of sand, the seat, the pier, the donkeys and the cheerful parade of late holiday-makers for her album. Not that she would need any reminder of this moment, it was already engraved on her memory for ever.

She sat down smiling into the September sunshine and closed her eyes. The key lay in her blazer pocket. For four days she had glanced at the dragging clock every few minutes, pushing the hands along with her eyes, but now time could slow down. In fact she needed time to think things out. Waiting for Paul.

Paul had been special right from the start. When she had arrived at Mendip School, the only new girl in the third year, everybody else had got their friends already. It had all been so sudden. Three months before she couldn't have imagined leaving Henbury Comprehensive and friends she had had since the infants. But Dad had been made redundant and then offered a job in Oman. Both her parents had been relieved, even pleased. Holly would probably enjoy boarding school life, her mother said. She must realise it wasn't easy for a man her father's age to get another job. In a matter of weeks it was all decided and the house let. By then her parents were not merely pleased, they were delighted with each other and the prospect ahead, hugging in corners like kids and then dashing to the shops for necessities not likely to be available in Oman. It seemed to Holly, pale and silent, that it was actually her thirteen-year-old self who had become redundant.

At first she had hated Mendip School, though she

managed to keep her letters to Oman cheerful. Her mother wrote back lyrically about miles of turquoise sea and almost white sand and smiling friendly people. Only Paul seemed to know by instinct how unhappy she was. He was a prefect in the fifth year then and on 'bed-put' twice a week. 'All right then, everybody?' he would say with the light shining on fair hair almost as white as the sand in Oman, smiling round with that special smile that freaked out the whole dormitory. You could tell the staff liked him too. 'Everybody settled?' No other duty prefect bothered like he did. Belinda for instance, 'Into bed, you lot,' she said switching out the light whether you had done your teeth or not.

From the first week Holly had loved him and by half-term he would sometimes sit on her bed and say, 'Okay, Holly?' Then they would talk for a few minutes while everybody else was still scurrying about and Holly would find the frozen lump of unhappiness inside her melting away. Love wasn't like the things they said in that book Angie gave her for Christmas, she thought, love was like a blowlamp. Dad had used one to unthaw a pipe once. At every bed-put she discovered something new, like Paul lived in Devon and had one brother and one sister and a labrador called Jet, collecting such fragments in her head like bright pennies.

By the second term Holly had stopped being unhappy and Ruth was her best friend and knew things that nobody else knew. How Holly had bought last year's school photo for fifty pence for instance, just to cut out Paul's face, though it was half the size of a postage stamp. Holly kept the photo pinned inside her blouse by day and under her pillow at night until she forgot and sent it to the laundry. Nothing was left but tiny flecks of white sticking to the navy blue. Ruth knew about that too.

'Don't forget Belinda,' Ruth said. Belinda was a weekly boarder and every Friday evening a Mercedes swept up the school drive to collect her. Paul always saw her off and stood there waving. Once Holly and Ruth had followed in the darkness and seen them kiss and Ruth had let out a disastrous snigger. 'Stupid little gits,' Belinda said looking round, but fortunately the Mercedes swept up the drive then and bore her away. Holly hoped and prayed they hadn't seen it was her but that night Paul smiled just as usual and his eyes were turquoise as the sea in Oman when he murmured, 'Okay, Holly?'

In those early days she recorded his smiles in her diary, counting them up at the end of each week. But that was before she had her camera. She photographed everything which made a marvellous excuse for getting lots of photographs with Paul somewhere in them. She didn't think it noticed until her aunt asked who the good-looking boy was who kept bobbing up and her cousin Angie giggled. Why ever had she confided in Angie? Holly went on taking photographs and even won third prize in the school magazine. At weekends she and Ruth walked across the Mendip Hills and always ended up at the farm down the road which had CIDER and CREAM TEAS on a board outside. Mrs Brown gave them double jam and cream and charged them half-price because they were from the school.

Then came the night of the disco. There was a disco at the school every Saturday night and by the end of the fourth year, Holly and Ruth mostly went. They were both fifteen by this time. Sometimes Paul was there. He was in the Lower Sixth now and he danced with various girls in his own form because Belinda had gone home. But suddenly at the beginning of the summer term he walked across and asked Holly to dance. She went bright pink as they went on the floor together. His body gliding and gyrating in time to the music just a few inches from hers was something else. But what she really liked was dancing with nobody in particular and watching Paul.

'You like Bros?' Paul said jerking his head towards the music. '"Drop The Boy," I really dig that single.'

'It's okay,' she said.

'And I like your dress,' he said. 'Really cosmic. Is it new?'

She shook her head. Apparently he hadn't noticed when she wore it for just about half of last year's discos. Aunt Olive thought dresses had to be outworn or outgrown. She struggled to think of something interesting, sparky, witty to say like other girls did but with Paul so close all the words took off from her head like a flock of birds.

'I got it in Hendon.'

'What?' he said not quite following because she had taken so long.

'This dress. I got it in Hendon.'

'Oh, right,' he said smiling such a wonderful smile it was like a present. It was almost too much dancing with Paul and even more too much when he asked her again. A waltz this time and quite smoochy, at least it was smoochy for some people. Paul held her away from him until Sebastian banged into them and said, 'She won't bite you, Paul. Promise you won't bite him, girlie?' Sebastian was always saying things like that.

'Good old Seb,' Paul said pulling her closer.

'Mm,' Holly said adjusting her view of Sebastian who she had always thought an embarrassing loudmouth up till then.

A moment later Paul said, 'Feel like a breath of fresh air?'

'Okay,' Holly said. It was May and chilly and quite natural that he should put his arm round her. The thump of the disco behind them drowned the thump of her heart. They were standing at the place where Belinda got into the car every Friday and Paul said, 'You know you're a bit special.'

'I'm not really,' she whispered.

'I think you are,' Paul said. 'Do you mind if I kiss you?'

'If you like...' she said. His lips brushed hers, soft as a moth in the darkness and then Mr Page came along swinging his torch. 'Break it up, you two,' he said. 'End of party.' Everybody grumbled about Pagey and his torch. He got his kicks that way, Sebastian said. Those who can do and those who can't watch.

Afterwards Paul continued to bestow his special smile on her but he never sat on her bed again and the next weekend he went home and the next after that he didn't go to the disco and the next he did but he didn't ask her to dance. Was it the way she kissed or what?

Towards the end of term everybody was talking about Sebastian's flat. His parents were divorced, that was nothing special at Mendip School, but only Sebastian boasted that ever since the divorce he could get any money he wanted out of his father. That summer Sebastian rented a flat in Weston-Super-Mare, a holiday letting.

'Like to come to the flat?' Paul had stopped suddenly in the corridor.

'What?' Holly said.

'Seb's flat on Saturday. I've got a key. Be a bit of a gas, right? Bit of an experience?'

'Okay,' she said.

'Brill,' said Paul. 'Meet you on the seat nearest the pier at three o'clock. And don't tell anyone, right?'

'Right,' she said and two days later there she was sitting on the seat near to the pier and there was Paul. He seemed different somehow, not so fair-haired, not so smiling, not himself any more.

The flat was in a grey Victorian house. The street door was open and they crept up the stairs. There was a brownish patterned stair carpet and brownish flowered wall-paper and a smell of cabbage. A woman came out of the basement and stared up. 'What you want?'

'We're friends of Sebastian Clarke,' Paul said.

'Oh, you are, are you?' she said. There was something nasty about her little tortoise eyes, Holly thought, but the woman seemed satisfied and disappeared back to the basement.

Paul unlocked the door of the flat and they went in. A hall and a large sitting room with a wrought-iron veranda overlooked the sea and was over-filled with furniture; two sofas and a motley assortment of armchairs. The rest of the flat was bathroom, kitchen and a small bed-room with a large double bed under a bright pink bed-spread.

'Shall I make a cup of tea?' Holly said. It was what her mother did when they arrived anywhere. She didn't seem like herself any more than Paul did.

'Right.' There proved to be half a dozen teabags in a tin labelled TEA but no milk. They sat on either end of the largest sofa sipping the hot bitter liquid and blinking at the shining sea. Suddenly there were footsteps on the stairs and Sebastian arrived with Candy from the Lower Sixth and a plastic flagon of cider.

'Hey, you turkeys, this a private snog-up or can anyone join?' he said splashing cider into glasses. 'Drink up.'

Holly had never drunk anything except half a glass of sherry at her cousin's wedding once, but she wasn't going to admit it. Besides, it might fill an aching hollowness inside. She drank cider and more cider; they all did. They were laughing a lot too because everything seemed to be funny. Then they went out to get fish and chips and Sebastian noticed the key cutting place. Nobody could call him a sexist pig, Sebastian said, and he had keys cut for Candy and Holly. 'Come whenever you want. Be my guest.' Then he had keys cut for all the girlies in the Lower Sixth. Sebastian walking off with a whole bagful of keys seemed funny too.

Holly clutched her key tight because the whole street was whirling. Then she was sick. Right there on the promenade. Weston was spinning like a top, sea above sky. She lay down right there and a ring of holiday makers gathered round her making helpful suggestions. It was awful but when she tried to get up she passed out. They had to phone the school and Mr Page fetched them in the minibus.

'Slaughter of the innocents,' he said. 'You lot ought to be ashamed of yourselves.'

'Don't say a thing,' Sebastian whispered into the petrol-flavoured darkness as they drove back. 'They can't chuck us out if they haven't got the evidence.'

Holly stayed in bed the next day and in the evening Mr Radley came to see her. 'Drinking cider, Holly, we can't have that, can we?' he said sternly and his grey eyes had lost their customary vagueness. 'Under-age drinking is against the law as well as against the whole ethos of the school as you well know. Where did the cider come from?'

Holly looked away and closed her lips firmly. She had let them down already, messed things up but she wasn't going to grass and get them chucked out as well. Mr Radley's questions went on and on and Holly went on shaking her head which made her feel sick.

'Did the cider come from the Browns' farm?' Mr Radley suggested and Holly nodded then. It was a way out, a way of stopping the questions. The Browns' farm was put out of bounds to the whole school at Monday morning assembly. Holly felt badly about that because Mrs Brown had been so good and besides she and Ruth would miss their cream teas.

'You all right?' Paul had said when he saw her in the corridor on Monday evening. Holly nodded.

'You didn't let on about the flat?' She shook her head. Some satisfaction in her silence under pressure gave her the boldness to say. 'Will you write to me this holiday?'

'Course I will,' Paul said smiling, though he did seem quite surprised. 'Give us your address?'

But he hadn't written. Her cousin, Angie, who was two years younger, ran to the post every morning announcing, 'Nothing for you,' or 'Only a letter from your mum,' in tones of exaggerated melancholy. Holly wore the key round her neck even at the swimming pool. It was a talking point and her favourite thing in the world was talking about Paul. She told Chris who lived in Hendon three houses down and she told a boy called Mike in the Isle of Wight as they wandered in the dark during a disco.

'Why don't you write to him?' Mike suggested. 'Maybe he's lost your address or something?' You could tell he wanted to get back to the disco.

It was the end of August when the postcard arrived from Spain. His parents had this villa in La Escala, Paul wrote, and Belinda was staying just around the corner and they were having a fantastic time.

'You got your wish,' Angie said. 'So you can just stop being such a wimp.'

'Only a postcard,' Holly said.

'Some people are just greedy,' Angie said.

A donkey brayed noisily and Holly sat up with a start. It was almost three o'clock and the tide had reached the top of the beach. Two children passed with sticks of pink candyfloss. If they went to the flat she would be different this time, not shy or anything. She was much more grown up after Chris, after Mike, you could say sophisticated.

'Have you got the key?' Paul said suddenly sitting down beside her. For once her sixth sense didn't seem to be working.

'Course I have,' Holly said smiling.

'Let's have it then?' He stood up then and threw the key as far as he could. It curled in an arc and plopped into the waves. 'Thank goodness for that,' he said brushing his hands. 'Last bit of evidence taken care of.'

Holly blushed. 'Aren't we going there?'

'Going there?' He seemed to see her for the first time. 'You out of your pram? We only took it for a week, I mean Seb only took it for a week. I had nothing to do with it, if Radley asks. I mean…we'll have some tea together if you like.' He glanced across the promenade gardens. 'Last term I was in line for head of school, head boy, the hot favourite, but now Mr Radley seems to think I had something to do with renting the flat…I mean your getting sick like that…'

'Sorry,' said Holly.

'Don't worry, kid,' Paul smiled kindly. 'I mean it's not

the end of the world. But if anybody asks you don't know anything about any flat and you never had a key and nor did I. It was Sebastian, right?'

'Right,' said Holly. She would lie for him, she would die for him. She wasn't exactly crying it was just tears were running down her face.

'Oh, don't...please...' Paul said helplessly. 'It was only a bit of a joke, wasn't it? I mean, you're a nice kid...sweet. But...well you don't know anything about any flat or any keys and nor does Belinda. It was just Sebastian. Okay?'

'But, Belinda *really* didn't...' Holly said, blowing her nose.

'I'd better go,' Paul said. 'Mind if we skip tea? Better we're not seen together. I mean it's a bit crucial just now. See you at supper then?'

He smiled his special smile and walked off towards the bus station.

Holly sat there for a long time, staring in front of her. The sea went out leaving an endless stretch of grey mud. The disco scene, the flat scene, the first scene with Paul played and replayed themselves in her head like a video on repeat. There seemed no reason why it should stop. But she got up in the end and got the bus too. Nobody seemed to notice how late she was.

'Where did you get to?' Ruth said, back from pot-holing and full of it.

'Nowhere,' Holly said and went to bed. On Monday Mr Radley announced that Belinda Turner was the new head girl and Paul Evans was second head. They both stood up and everybody clapped and cheered for a full two minutes. It was a popular choice because the whole school knew about Paul and Belinda.

Holly expected to be miserable for the rest of her life, but after a day or two she found she wasn't. She went on taking photographs and Mr Page put her name up for the Photographers' Club and a postcard came from Chris. Holly felt new and scared like a hatched chick but she also felt free. Each day belonged to her and she no longer wanted to hurry it away. She had changed and Paul was changing too. His hair had become just ordinary fair and his eyes an ordinary greyish blue and his smile wasn't all that special any more. Not when he smiled at her anyway. Perhaps he blamed her for the disappointment of being only second head. Anyway by the end of the school year he was just another person. Almost.

'Lord dismiss us with thy blessing,' everybody sang at the last assembly and Holly stood in a line and shook hands just like everybody else and said, 'Goodbye, Belinda. Goodbye, Paul, and good luck.'

Cal
Jean Ure

Linda's blood starts on its familiar surging, her heart hammers in its cage. She cranes forward on her seat, peering out through the windows of the bus… it *is* Cal! This time it really is! Please say that it is! This time, let it be him…

Frantically she rubs her hand across the glass where her breath has smeared it. Now she can't see him, he has disappeared, swallowed up in the crowds of people thronging the High Street. Panic sets in. She starts to her feet, striving for a better view. Cal, where are you? Where have you gone? She can't lose him now! Not now!

There he is, up ahead. Striding out, in that way that he had. Shoulders back, head held high … Cal! She would recognise that walk of his anywhere, even after all this time … Cal, she cries, wait for me!

As she leaps for the stairs the bus jolts to a sudden standstill, throwing her back on to her heels. She regains her balance, glances again out of the window, checking, just to make sure … *is* it Cal? Or is it yet another look-alike?

She falls back. She must be wary, bide her time, let the bus move on, take another look. She has been caught too often. It's not the embarrassment which bothers her; it's the pain she can't take. The wrenching agony as it hits her – this is not Cal! It has happened so often, you would think she would grow used to it, would arm herself against the disappointment, but she never does. It tears her apart every time.

But Cal is out there! Somewhere, he is out there! One

day she will find him again, and then she will tell him, what she never had the chance to tell him before ... Cal, I'm sorry! Forgive me!

In her heart she has long forgiven him for the pain he has caused: she needs desperately to know that he has forgiven her. That is why she goes on searching; that, plus the fact that she loves him so. Time has not diminished the strength of her feelings. She knows that it never will: her love for Cal will be with her always.

Now she is no longer on the bus. She has to get down there, get after him, chasing phantoms on her own two feet, flying up the High Street, dodging through the shoppers, through the tourists ... Cal, wait for me! Please, wait for me!

He is there, still striding ahead, within shouting distance, but her mouth, as it always does, has gone dry; she tries to call but no sound comes. Perhaps because she is scared that yet again he will turn and look at her and his face will be that of a stranger. Black faces are two a penny these days in the High Street in Kensington. This is why her heart leaps so often and her disappointments are so cruel and come so frequently. Times have changed since she first met Cal. When Linda was a child she and Ben had had to be told, very sternly, 'Not to stare' if they saw a black person on the tube.

'Staring is rude,' their mother had said. 'How would you like it if people sat and stared at you?'

All very well, but how could you not, when the only black people you had ever seen, almost, had been in pictures, in books about Africa? It was all so long ago. So long, long ago! Such an eternity of yearning – such an intensity of pain ... Cal, my beloved, do you still ache for me as I ache for you? Or have you forgotten me, where you have been? I think I couldn't bear it if you had forgotten me; yet equally I couldn't bear it if I thought you had suffered. We never knew, my darling, did we, that hot summer's day in another age, what cruel blows the future held? If I could only go back, just for one moment, just to be with you again ...

'Linda, Linda! Come quick!' cried Ben. He scuttled across the kitchen like an eager crab, grabbing her by the hand and pulling her back out with him into the sunbaked garden. 'There's black people!'

'Black people? Where?'

'Down the bottom, through the bushes ... come!'

Down the bottom through the bushes was where the back yards of the Victorian terrace known as Foulsham's Cottages met the one-and-a-half acres of garden which surrounded Fairlawns. Mr Kilroy, the children's father, did things in the City – Linda was never quite sure what, possibly she had never asked, since doing things in the City was not the type of activity which interested her, she was more intrigued by famous film stars and actors – but whatever it was it obviously, as Ben was to remark in later years, 'brought home the bacon'. The Kilroys, without any doubt, were several cuts above the humble inhabitants of Foulsham's Cottages.

Not that the Cottages were slum territory: Mother would never have stood for that. But the women wore wrap-around floral aprons and could sometimes be seen with curlers in their hair, and the men did menial clerical jobs in offices run by people like Linda's father, and the children, unless they were clever enough to win scholarships, went to the local council school and mixed with 'all sorts', meaning slum children and children from the orphanage, with nits in their hair and very likely body lice as well. And now there were *black people*.

'Through there!' said Ben, and dived off into the bushes. Linda followed, bending double and trying to keep the branches out of her hair and the twigs from tearing her skirt. Mother didn't care for her playing in the bushes. Ben was considered too young to know better, being only twelve, and anyway he was a boy; boys were allowed to grub around and get dirty. Linda was sixteen, going on seventeen, and expected to comport herself like a young lady. Didn't they send her to Miss Gresham's especially for the purpose? It cost a lot of money, did Miss Gresham's – 'But we want you to have exactly the same opportunity as your brother.' Mother and Father were quite enlightened in some ways. Next year Pam would also go to Miss Gresham, starting in the infants' section known as The Homestead. Pam was the baby of the family. 'An Afterthought,' said Mother. Sometimes that was what they called her: the Afterthought.

Ben had wriggled his way through to the fence which separated the gardens. He turned, waiting for Linda.

'Hurry! Quick!' He mouthed the words at her, jigging up and down in his eagerness to show her.

Linda squeezed herself free of the bushes. Obediently she applied her eye to the place where he was pointing, a knothole in the fence, about halfway up. Ben danced triumphantly at her side. 'See?'

It was even as he had said: black people had moved into one of Foulsham's Cottages. They were there, now, in the narrow back yard, three of them, doing something with garden tools. A tall black boy, digging with a spade; a medium-size black girl, down on her haunches, shaking earth through a sieve; and a smaller black girl, on her knees, scraping with a trowel. Linda stared in fascination, her one eye glued to the hole.

'Are they still there?' whispered Ben.

She nodded, absorbed.

'Let's have another look!'

'In a minute.' She wasn't ready to give up her post just yet. She had never seen any black people so close before. She wondered whether they were brother and sisters and how old they were. The bigger girl, she thought, must be about thirteen or fourteen, the younger one nine or ten. She couldn't see the boy properly, he had his back to her.

Suddenly, as she watched, the boy picked up the spade with one hand, pitched it deep into the earth, and with an air of some purpose straightened up. She backed away, in a hurry. She knew he couldn't see her through the knothole, it was far too small, but still you felt guilty, spying on people as they went about their lawful business.

She turned to Ben – and discovered, horrified, that in his impatience to take another look he had hoisted himself up the fence and was peering over the top of it, in absolutely full view of the black people should they chance to turn in his direction.

'*Ben!*' She hissed it at him. He turned his head.

'What?'

'Get down!'

Too late: another pair of hands were already grasping the top of the fence, followed almost immediately by the head and shoulders of the boy who had been digging.

'Are you looking for something?' he said.

It was such a shock! He spoke English, just like anybody else. Ben gawped, grew red and slithered back down the fence. It was left to Linda to invent a likely-sounding excuse.

'Our ball,' she said. 'I'm sorry, you must think us very rude. We were playing cricket, you see, and –'

'You hit a six.'

Right over the bushes and the tops of the trees. It would have been a jolly good hit. Cal himself might have been capable of it. Linda certainly wouldn't, nor twelve-year-old Ben.

Cal smiled kindly at her. 'You ought to play for England,' he said.

She blushed; not so much because she had been caught out as because he had smiled. And because his voice was soft and lilting, not harsh and clipped like English voices, and she had never had a boy smile at her in quite that way before.

'What number do you bat at?' he said.

'She doesn't bat at any number!' Ben couldn't resist it. Boasting would be his downfall one of these days. Or maybe he thought he was helping. 'I'm the one that hits sixes, not her!'

'Oh?' One eyebrow quizzically lifted. 'What's your name? Jack Hobbs?'

'Ben Kilroy,' said Ben. 'What's yours?'

'Cal Kennedy.'

'How do you do?' said Ben, from the bottom of the fence. 'This is my sister, Linda.' Ben had been well brought up: he knew it was only polite to make introductions.

'Hello, Ben. Hello, Linda.' Cal leaned over, reaching an arm down towards them. Much embarrassed, Linda took the hand he was offering her. It was the first time she had ever spoken to a black person, never mind touched one.

She wondered what Mother would say. Mother was

very strict about not conversing with strangers, especially men, though whether Cal would count as a man or as a boy she couldn't be sure. She thought he was probably about the same age as herself, but while girls were expected to turn into young ladies the very minute they reached sixteen, boys seemed to be allowed to go on being boys for practically ever. Until they went to war; war finished all that. When they went to war they had to grow up whether they liked it or not. Marching off like big real men to prove themselves ... to drop their bombs and fire their guns, to maim and slaughter and indiscriminately destroy. And all in the sacred name of democracy. Even Cal. Oh, Cal! Even you ...

Linda's breath comes in gasps as she fights to free herself from the encumbrance of the crowd in the High Street. Cal is pulling away from her, she can just catch the occasional glimpse of him, still striding ahead. She redoubles her efforts; her lungs feel as if they are bursting. People tut and mutter, wondering what the hurry is. Some step out of her way, others, resentful, bar her passage. She pushes and shoves, not caring. She will even resort to kicking, to using her elbows, if necessary. Cal is still there, and this time she knows she is not mistaken. It is a feeling she has. This time, when she catches him up, it *will* be Cal ...

'It *was* him, wasn't it?' said Mother. She looked at Linda gravely. 'The boy at the end of the garden?'

She would never call him by his name; not even when they had been neighbours for a whole year. But Mother didn't count the inhabitants of Foulsham's Cottages as neighbours, specially if they were black. It wasn't that there was anything *wrong* with being black, and certainly one mustn't stare, because staring was rude in any circumstances, and besides they had their feelings just the same as anyone else; but having said that one had said quite as much as one need, if not indeed a great deal more, and surely Linda must have known that if she had gone to Mother and asked permission to do what she had done the answer would have been no?

'But we weren't "doing" *any*thing!' Linda let it burst out of her, aggressively. She didn't usually talk to Mother in such a rude tone of voice, but she was feeling desperate, and hard-done-by: that hateful old harridan, Mrs Anstruther from across the way, had seen her and Cal walking hand in hand on Sunday afternoon in Hyde Park. Mother had been deeply shocked. She had not thought Linda capable of such duplicity.

'It's not so much what you did or didn't do as the fact that you saw fit to lie to me.' Linda had said she was going round to Barbara Bailey's to play records. She had supposedly been going round to Barbara Bailey's rather a lot just lately; every Sunday afternoon for the last three months, in fact. Now Mother knew where it was that she had really been, and who it was she had really been with, and Mother was going to speak to Father and there was going to be one almighty row.

'You knew perfectly well,' said Mother, 'that you were doing wrong.'

'What's wrong,' sobbed Linda, 'with just going for a walk?'

'What is wrong is that you lied to me!'

They tried to make out it was the lying which was so bad, but Linda knew, and Ben knew, though the

Afterthought was still too young, that it was Linda walking hand in hand with a black person that had angered them. It didn't matter that Cal went to the local boys' grammar school and wore a smart green uniform with silver piping and had learnt to speak nicely (without dropping his aitches, which was very important to Mother and Father), they had already warned Ben, very early on, 'I don't think we want you climbing over the fence into other people's gardens, darling. It's not very nice, is it?'

They hadn't thought to warn Linda, and certainly she hadn't climbed *over* the fence, though she had on several occasions hoisted herself up and sat on it; and even now, now that they had discovered about the walks in Hyde Park, they didn't know about the secret meetings on the way home from school or the long winter kisses, her and Cal huddled in shop doorways, in the early evening dark. She was the only girl in the whole of the Gresham's sixth form with a regular boyfriend. The other girls kept asking her, 'What's it like? Being kissed by a black person?' She didn't think of Cal as a black person any more. You were just Cal, my darling …

She is free of the crowds now. She is running, running, running. The blood pounds in her ears, small slivers of silver like silver fish darting across her eyes … wait for me. Cal! Wait for me!

Suddenly she stumbles. Her heart, in that moment, seems to stop. The shoals of silver burst into a searing sunset of vivid reds and orange. She tries to rise, but her legs buckle beneath her. She can run no more: she feels that she is done. Cal! she cries. Help me!

Some of Cal's remembered strength flows into her. She fancies that she feels his arms about her, supporting her, lifting her. She knows that it cannot be, for Cal, now, is almost out of sight; but it gives her the will to carry on. Just a few yards more ... I'm coming, Cal! I'm coming!

'We'll come and visit you at half-term,' her mother said, as she saw her off at Waterloo station, bound for the new posh boarding school they were banishing her to in the depths of rural Buckinghamshire.

'Going to be finished!' jeered the girls at Gresham's, envious because they would have liked to go and be finished as well. Linda had put up a fight, but Mother was adamant.

'It's for your own good,' she said. Girls, she might have added, who cannot be trusted ... but they were pretending it was nothing to do with the incident in the Park. They were blaming what Father called 'the state of play' in Europe. It was 1939 and there was going to be war soon, everyone was saying so; it was only a matter of time.

'I shall be able to rest easier at night,' said Mother, 'knowing you're safe in the country.' What she meant was safe from Cal, not from Hitler. After all, what about Pam? Ben was already away at boarding school, but nobody was talking of sending Pam into the country.

'Pam is too little,' said Mother. 'I shall take her down to Devon, when the time comes.'

So why couldn't Linda have waited till the time came? Because Linda had been deceitful and held hands with a black person, and things must be put a stop to before they went too far. The last words Mother spoke, as the train huffed and puffed and got up steam preparing to depart, were: 'Remember, Linda, what you've promised us.'

They had forced her into it. She had had to promise that she would do 'nothing behind their back' – which meant not communicating with Cal in any shape manner or form. Mother had nothing against black people, and neither had Father. Linda wasn't to suppose that they were in any way prejudiced. But, 'Each to his own,' said Father. And, 'I think you know what we mean,' said Mother. 'Otherwise why would you have lied to us? If you hadn't felt guilty, you would have seen no need to lie.'

And so they had made her promise, but it had been a promise extracted under duress and Linda had no intention of keeping it. They soon found a way of corresponding; there were always ways, if you looked hard enough. Because Linda was fairly certain that her mail was being subjected to scrutiny by Miss Moorehead, who had obviously been warned by Mother, she enlisted the help of a girl called Derrica Ferbane who thought it the most romantic thing in the world to act as a letterbox for star-crossed lovers. She thought it even more romantic when Linda showed her the photograph of her and Cal (taken by a street photographer one day, as they walked in Hyde Park) which Linda kept pressed against her bosom, inside her liberty bodice.

'Oh! Isn't he *gorgeous?* Linda, I could *melt!*'

Derrica was a bit silly, perhaps, but Linda could put up with a bit of silliness for the sake of Cal's letters. *For love is heaven and heaven is love*, he wrote, quoting Walter Scott. And, *Love all alike, no season knows, nor clime Nor hours, days, months, which are the rags of time.*

That was John Donne. Cal was very well read – better, in fact, than Linda. He was hoping to go to university and take a degree in English, something which would have astounded Mother and Father had they known.

When Derrica Ferbane, one morning at breakfast, excitedly smuggled her a letter from Cal, in which he asked her as a matter of urgency whether she could slip out of school and meet him in the nearby town, she had no hesitation in replying that she could. She would be discovered and she would be censured and very possibly might even be expelled, but what did she care? It was September; the long-expected war had finally been declared two weeks before, and they would probably all be dead soon, killed by gas or Hitler's bombs. Linda didn't share the general view that war was a necessary evil. She and Cal had discussed it often during their walks in the Park. They had agreed that they were pacifists. No power on earth would make them take arms against their fellow men.

'In the First World War,' said Linda, 'they sent white feathers to conscientious objectors.'

Cal had said he reckoned he could stand a few white feathers: 'Sticks and stones may break my bones, but a few white feathers surely aren't going to hurt me.'

And then he had sprung it on her, that day in the town. He had enlisted, and she couldn't believe it. That Cal of all people would turn his back on his principles, would be scared of a few white feathers. But he had said, 'They think badly enough of us already,' meaning people like Mother and Father, 'they think we shouldn't be over here, they say we don't belong, that it's not our country… I don't want to give them grounds for accusing us,' he said, 'of being too cowardly to go and fight, of not being patriotic.' And all she could think of was that she couldn't bear it, she just couldn't bear it if anything should happen to Cal, and she had screamed at him in her selfishness that by doing what he had done he had shown himself to be more of a coward than by refusing to do it; a moral coward and a hypocrite, and that what people thought about him mattered more to him than she did, and I wouldn't listen, oh, Cal! I wouldn't listen when you tried to explain to me, that what you were doing you were doing for us, for you and me, that I meant all the world to you.

'I love you,' you said, 'more than life itself ...' and I never said that I loved you back, I never told you that my heart was split asunder with the pain of our parting, I never even kissed you goodbye ... Cal! Oh, Cal! If I could just speak to you one more time ...

Linda stumbles, gasping, through the gates of the Park. The man whom she has chased the whole length of Kensington High Street in the belief that he is Cal remains ahead of her, just tantalisingly out of reach. She makes one last great effort – 'Cal!' she calls, and this time her voice obeys her. It is not very loud, but loud enough. The man stops. Slowly he turns.

'Cal,' whispers Linda. Cal doesn't say anything, but his arms open wide to receive her.

'Just half an hour too late,' says the pleasant young doctor in her white coat. 'Such a shame, when you've come all that way ... Australia, was it?'

'Canada,' says Pam. She touches a finger to her sister's cheek, pale as snow against the starched hospital linen. 'Was it – quite easy?'

'Very easy,' says the doctor. 'She simply went to sleep and didn't wake. She was a bit distressed at one point, she kept asking for someone called Cal ... we checked the records but we couldn't find anyone by that name, then one of the nurses discovered this, in her locker.'

The doctor hands Pam a yellowing photograph,

postcard-size, showing a young couple wearing the clothes of long ago and strolling hand in hand against a background of trees.

'If you turn it over –' says the doctor.

Pam turns it over. In her sister's writing she sees, *Cal and me in the Park: July 1939*. 'Cal!' she says. She sounds surprised, yet realises in fact that she isn't.

'We gave it to your sister to hold,' says the doctor, 'and it seemed to comfort her. She sank quite peacefully just a few minutes later.'

'I wish I could have been in time to say goodbye,' says Pam, as she leaves the hospital with her sixteen-year-old daughter, Elaine. 'But maybe she wouldn't have known me.'

Elaine takes the photograph out of the small plastic bag of possessions which the hospital have given to her mother as next of kin. 'He looks nice,' she says, referring to Cal. 'What happened to him?'

'Cal was killed in the war,' says Pam, 'very early on.'

Elaine doesn't believe in war; not at any cost. There is no cause so great, she thinks, that men should kill for it.

'What a waste,' she says. She shakes her head, so that her heavy blonde hair sways to and fro like a curtain. 'Was that the reason, do you suppose, that Aunt Linda never married?'

'I've often wondered,' says Pam. 'Not that she ever talked about it.'

'So that was another waste … poor Aunt Linda!'

'She's happy now,' says Pam. She takes the photograph from Elaine and slips it back into the plastic bag along with the rest of the possessions – the watch, the dentures, the purse, the pension book. A packet of faded letters tied with a ribbon. 'She's with Cal.'

Icebreaker

Pete Johnson

I'm something of an expert on horny women. In fact, I have spent a large part of my fourteen years compiling – and up-dating – lists on this vital subject. These lists have gone all round my school (four hundred and fifty-two sex-starved boys) and generally given much satisfaction, until yesterday. That was when Martin Adams said, 'But you've missed out …' and then he said her name.

'She's beyond horny,' I said, before quickly changing the subject. Martin Adams, being a lower form of pond life, didn't know what I was talking about. But to be fair, 'beyond horny' is a new category – and one in which there can only ever be one name. Deborah Harper is the very definition of gorgeous: blonde, blue-eyed, with a knock-out smile, and a brilliant personality. She also never wore a bra. She was, in fact, everything I looked for in a teacher.

The news that Mrs Spacey, an evil old witch who used to make all her own dresses (horrible flowered ones) and shouted at you all the time, was away ill, led to much rejoicing. But when her replacement shimmered into view, an awe-struck silence fell upon the room. For never in the history of the world had a woman under the age of ninety-four been allowed within a hundred yards of our school. Let alone this vision of beauty.

'Hello, my name's Miss Harper and I'm taking over Mrs Spacey's English classes while she's away. Now, I'll try and help you all I can. All right?'

No one trusted themselves to reply. We just gazed in

wonderment at the way her chest filled her top. Then she sat on the desk. Her legs were hidden beneath one of those tight skirts. But when she crossed her legs you caught a quick flash of knees. and she crossed and uncrossed her legs quite a lot that lesson, saying things like, 'You're a very quiet class, aren't you?'

For no one answered any of her friendly questions. In fact, I don't remember anyone actually moving. Well, how can you when you've got what feels like a lead weight down your trousers?

During her second lesson the low life found a voice. She was talking about our exam text, *Pride and Prejudice*, and then asked, 'Any questions so far?'

'Yeah, will you go out with me?' Martin Adams suddenly called out.

Martin Adams is an ugly morsel of humanity who's always got to be in on everything. I mean you can be making a joke on another table to him which he can't even hear properly but he'll still laugh his zits off at it.

Martin Adams is always making stupid cracks and most teachers just brush him away. But Miss Harper didn't. Instead she blushed and dropped her pen and made me want to punch Martin Adams in the face. Especially when he went on, 'I'll pick you up tonight then. We can go to Cally's,' (a local night-club very popular with hammer-heads like him).

She looked as if she were about to drop her pencil again and my heart ached for her but then she lowered her voice and said, 'I'm sorry, I don't like toy boys.'

We all laughed far more enthusiastically than her little joke demanded. Especially me. And Martin Adams had to content himself with whispering, 'She's screaming for it,' which she very wisely pretended not to hear.

Still, her discipline was a little shaky and it was obvious she needed a champion. I quickly decided there was only one person mature enough for the job. So when she started asking questions about *Pride and Prejudice*, my hand shot up every time. And she seemed so concerned that we knew nothing about the book (all my answers were wrong), that I began to feel quite ashamed.

'But why don't you like *Pride and Prejudice*?' she asked.

'Because it's a girls' book', replied one guy.

'Oh, really,' she leaned forward and one of her buttons looked as if it were about to spring open. The class nearly fainted with excitement.

'But why is it a girls' book?' she asked.

'Because it's just about people meeting and getting married,' said a guy in the front.

'And only women get married, do they?' she said, flashing this dead cheeky smile at us. 'I'll tell you what,' she went on, 'I'm going to ask you boys to write me a love story. I mean it couldn't be more appropriate, could it, with Valentine's Day next Monday. Now it can be any kind of love story ...'

I was the last to leave her class. 'Thank you for a very good lesson,' I said.

She looked up, startled but pleased.

'You really made it interesting.'

Her face lit up with pleasure now. 'Well thank you, I try and do things in a fun way.'

I slowly walked towards her. For this beat of time it was just her and me. And I had to stretch this moment out as long as I could.

'I was just wondering, did Jane Austen write any other books?'

'Yes, she did. Five other novels actually.'

'Oh, great,' I said. 'Brilliant.'

Actually I think I rather overdid the enthusiasm for she had a little smile on her face as she said, 'If you're that keen I could lend you one of her books.'

'Oh, yes please,' I said. This could be the start of all sorts of private intimate chats. 'I'd be really grateful.'

'You enjoy Jane Austen's books then?' she said, that little smile on her face again.

'Oh, yes,' I said, then remembering a word she'd used earlier, 'especially her irony.'

Behind us the door kept bursting open, a new class was eager to spill in. She was smiling broadly at me now. 'I'll bring the book for you tomorrow then, Scott.'

She knows my name!

I exist for her. And I'll bet she doesn't know the name of many in my class. I grinned back at her, suddenly, wildly happy.

I rushed home, eager to write my love story for her, but I was interrupted by my girlfriend. Sally and I met in the back row of the cinema two months ago. It was when all my mates had suddenly acquired girlfriends. So all around me people were groping and moaning furiously – all except one girl. She had just finished with someone and looked miserable all evening. I wasn't sure if me speaking to her would make her even more miserable, so in the end I did nothing. But the second week I saw her there, I finally gathered up my courage and spoke to her. The following week we sat together. And two months later we still team up once or twice a week. It's nothing serious but it's all right.

Recently she's had this craze for ice-skating and keeps dragging me along. I hate it there, it's a real poseur's paradise. Tonight, as usual, Sally had her hair all gelled back, even though I said doing that was really bad for her hairline and she'll be bald by the time she's thirty. Sally's a bit girly actually, like tonight. She had on her baggy jeans with a stupid little picture of Fred Flintstone on and was strutting around with her skates over her shoulder. She doesn't exactly skate round her handbag, but she comes close to that.

This evening, though, she hardly went on the ice, just kept disappearing to the loo, which suited me. For I stood on the edge listening to the music and picturing Miss Harper and I skating together, only not here, the ice was too lumpy and dangerous. No, somewhere secluded and far away. And Miss Harper would be whirling around, not on skates but on those kinky leather boots she wears to school.

We didn't have English on Wednesday but there were dramatic news flashes about her all day – her buttons came undone twice! I waited until the end of school before collecting my book from her. I'd wanted to make sure we wouldn't be disturbed.

She was packing away some exercise books but as soon as she saw me she cried, 'Oh, your book. It's in the car, can you wait a minute?'

I'll wait forever for you, I thought, but I just nodded, then added conversationally, 'Have a good day?'

'Hectic. Very hectic,' she said. 'Some of my classes are very excitable.'

Then she started piling exercise books into another bag.

'May I carry these for you?' I asked.

'Why, thank you, Scott,' she said, and I felt that rush of

pleasure I always got when she said my name.

We walked to her car, chatting and laughing, just as if we were a real couple going out together. Her car was really flash too, a black MG sports car. 'I am impressed,' I said.

'Don't be. It's a real mess inside – and it needs a wash.'

'I'll clean it for you, if you like,' I said.

She smiled. 'How much do you charge?'

'Oh, I'm dead expensive. But for you – no charge.'

For a moment she looked at me as if she really liked me, then said briskly, 'Well, we'll see. Anyway, here's your bedtime reading. It's called *Emma* by Jane Austen, and it's just packed full of irony,' she was smiling again at me now.

I watched her put on her black driving gloves, then waved her off. I wondered where she was going. She obviously wouldn't be going out tonight, not with two bags full of marking. Then I opened my copy of *Emma* and just inside in green ink was her signature – Deborah Harper. Suddenly the book was very precious and even though it had really small print and looked pretty dodgy, I was determined to read every word.

Back home the telephone was screaming to be answered. It was Sally. 'I've got something to tell you,' she said. 'Oh, Scott, I'm sorry, but I've met someone else.'

It turned out he worked at the café at the ice-skating rink. She'd been seeing him for a while but wasn't sure. Only now she was.

'I should have told you before,' she said. 'I feel dreadful.'

'Don't,' I said. 'It's all right provided you don't say can we still be friends. I can't stand it when people say that. I am still your friend of course.'

'Oh, yes, Scott, and I'm still yours,' she said. 'And thank you for being so good about it. I'm sure you'll find someone else.'

'Actually, I already have.'

'Oh, who?' her voice had chilled a bit.

'Well it's nothing definite ...'

'Do I know her?'

'No, I don't think so. She's called Deborah – Deborah Harper.'

To cheer myself up – I was amazed at how upset I was by Sally finishing with me – I began my love story. The first page was a description of Deborah. She'd surely recognise herself when she read it. Well I didn't care. In fact, I wanted her to know.

Then, on the second page, I was taking her skating when suddenly she came shooting towards me with her arms outstretched – and sent me hurtling backwards on to the base of my spine. All at once I was falling into the cold, murky depths of the lake. I think I described that part really well. I liked my ending too. That was where the immense cold stiffened my arms and legs so much I couldn't move. All I could do was gaze upwards at Deborah, her face contorted with agony.

'Forgive me,' she cried. 'Forgive me.'

I couldn't reply. All I could do was smile heroically. Until the end when I disappeared completely, killed by too much love.

It was called, *Love Kills*.

I was going to hand in my essay to Deborah on Friday, give her something of mine to read over the weekend. But in the end I lost my nerve and decided to hand it in on Monday with everyone else. Deborah and I had two conversations about Jane Austen's *Emma*, though. I sat up till half past two, reading it. Once you get into it – well it's still quite boring actually. Not that I told Deborah that!

Then, after school, I did something I've never done before – looked at the Valentine cards, trying to decide which one I would send Deborah. There was one which said simply, 'You open up my heart' which I liked. But I decided to have a last look around the shops tomorrow before finally choosing.

Then, as usual, I went to the pictures. Only this time I was relegated to the row where guys who haven't any girlfriends sit. I thought of Sally, with that toe-rag at the skating rink. What had he got that I hadn't? How could she prefer him to me?

To cheer myself up I imagined Deborah and me at the cinema. We'd share a box of liqueurs as we watched one of those culty foreign films with sub-titles and I'd have my arm around Deborah and then we'd plunge into a kiss that went on and on ...

Suddenly this guy next to me said, 'Miss Harper,' and I jumped in the air, for it was just as if he'd been peering right into my mind.

Then I realised he was pointing down the cinema.

'I've just seen her,' he said.

'What, here?' I exclaimed, excited but disbelieving. This seemed just too wonderful to be true. Then I sped out of my seat and pushed my way through the group of boys from my school which had gathered round her. Seeing any teacher out of school was interesting but seeing Deborah...

And there she was, wearing a black leather jacket just as I'd imagined. In fact, she was exactly as I'd pictured her. Except for the fact she had her arm around another man.

And then she saw me and she smiled – and her smile was like a knife going through me. For all the time she was smiling at me she kept her arm tightly around him. I thought it was the most obscene thing I'd ever seen. Especially when he took over the conversation, yarning on about her car breaking down and how he'd had to sort everything out. And she kept looking at him like he was someone really exciting. He was about as exciting as a three day old plate of rice pudding.

I desperately wanted to pull away from this scene. But I couldn't move. Even my facial muscles seemed to have frozen up. So I just stood there, trapped in a nightmare, which kept on getting worse and worse. For he started talking about their engagement next month and the ring he was going to buy her. Then he asked if any of the boys here were planning to get engaged soon and showing all his black teeth as he said it.

What's she doing with that fart-face? And why doesn't she want me?

At last the lights dimmed, everyone went back, reluctantly, to their seats and I rushed out of the cinema and into the smoky rawness of the night. I was raging now. I wanted to grab hold of fart-face and bite things off him. I was desperate to lash out at something. Finally, in a frenzy of frustration, I ripped all the buttons off my black shirt.

Ever since I wore that shirt everything had gone wrong. So it was clearly an unlucky shirt. Back home I deposited the remains of it in the bin, tears of anger still on my face.

*

All weekend I could think only of her and fart-face. And the anger seemed to go deeper and deeper inside me. Until that anger had hardened into something which lay on top of my stomach. And whenever I moved I could feel it there, rock hard. Only one thought gave me any pleasure – my revenge!

Monday morning *she* breezed in, all happy. 'I love your sexy way,' was written on the board (she promptly rubbed it off, laughing nervously), and a Valentine card awaited her on the desk. Her hand shook slightly as she showed it to us. 'Don't open this card unless you love me,' was on the front, while inside the card it said, 'I love you too.' And all at once she was smiling at me. She thought I'd sent it.

'That delightful, romantic card,' quick smile at me again, 'has put me in the mood to hear some of your love stories. They are finished aren't they 4C?'

There were the usual excuses before she said, 'Now come on, someone must have finished his love story. Don't be shy now.'

Slowly I raised my hand. 'I've finished mine if you'd like to hear it.'

'Thank you, Scott. I'd love to hear it.'

She sat back, ready to be enthralled. Even now I had to admit she looked beautiful, heart-stoppingly beautiful. But then I thought of her and fart-face and that sharp, stabbing pain plunged through me again.

I brought out my essay, not my soppy skating story – that was thrown into the back of my cupboard – but the one I'd dashed off this morning. And then I read: 'There's this man who lives in a house with no windows. The letter-box is his only bit of light and air. But then on

Valentine's Day he gets so many cards that his letter-box gets choked up so he can't breathe and dies. The End.'

The class laugh while she stares at me, stunned and bewildered.

'Oh, Scott, I am so disappointed,' she said.

'Oh, Scott,' mimicked Martin Adams, and there was a faint but unmistakable stirring of restlessness from the rest of the room. But she didn't seem aware of any of that. She was too busy mourning her disappointment in me. She even went and stood by my desk, as if still unable to take in what I'd written. She picked up my scrap of paper, scrutinising it, shaking her head and looking at me, while I felt a hotness in my eyes as if I were about to cry which quickly turned to fury. How dare she be disappointed in me. She had no right to do that.

And suddenly the class erupted into laughter. For my desk was slowly rising. 'Scott, what are you doing?' she said.

'Sorry, Miss, but I can't control myself when you get near me.'

I was pushing my desk right up in the air now.

'Down boy, down,' called Martin Adams.

More laughter and then Martin Adams's desk started rising too, while he made strange, groaning noises.

'Stop. Stop this at once,' she cried.

But her voice was just a little too high, her tone a little too hysterical to stop anything. Instead other desks started rising and there was a sense of release, of things suddenly being said, as rude comments kept being blurted out; the lesson was a shambles.

As I left she was sitting behind her desk, looking lost and forlorn. Again I wanted to cry but then another surge of fury swept through me as I hurled her copy of Jane

Austen's *Emma* on to the desk. 'It was crap,' I said. Then I quickly turned away and left.

An hour later I collapsed with a blinding headache. I was sent home. My mother thought it might be the start of flu. I felt awful. The smoky rawness of Friday night seemed to have lodged itself in the back of my throat. While my headache roared on and on.

For two days I lay in bed covered in cold, freezing sweat, drifting in and out of dreams about her. But even in my dreams she was always with fart-face. Until one time I just saw her face staring at me and she looked so puzzled, so wounded, that an ache welled up in me. I hadn't meant to hurt her. But I had. In fact I'd... Just what had I done? I had to see her again, to explain, to apologise, to beg her forgiveness.

So, on Friday morning, despite Mum's protesting, I returned to the scene of my crime. It was English first lesson and I was late, so I charged into the classroom and then froze in horror.

'What are you doing here?' I yelled.

'How dare you come into my classroom like that,' cried Mrs Spacey. 'Get out – now.'

But I could only blink at her disbelievingly. Where was she, Miss Harper, Deborah? She couldn't just disappear like that. But she had. It turned out that Spacey had been back since Wednesday – and in an even fouler mood than usual. And afterwards she really gave me the verbals. I said nothing, just listened with bowed head. I needed a favour.

Finally I asked most politely, 'Mrs Spacey, could I trouble you for Miss Harper's address please?'

She spluttered with astonishment. 'Miss Harper's

address – why?' Then she stared at me curiously.

'Well I never handed in my essay…'

'I'll mark any work you have produced. I'm sure Miss Harper has far more important things to do than read your outpourings.'

'I think she'd like to see this essay though.'

'Oh, really – why? Where is it? Show it to me.'

'Well it's not here and actually, it's private.'

Saying it was private was a cock up of the first order, for now Spacey was bristling with anger and suspicion.

'Private. How can it be private?'

I tried levelling with her. 'I have to apologise to her. I didn't behave very well in her class.'

'I'm sure Miss Harper has forgotten about you long ago,' snapped Spacey.

I was sweating again. 'Mrs Spacey, I do need to write to her. It really is important. So please, could you …'

'I would never give out a member of staff's address to a pupil,' she said. 'Never,' before sweeping past me.

Desperate now I ran to the office. The secretary there was quite sympathetic but very firm. She couldn't give out any staff addresses. And she didn't even know if she had Miss Harper's address anyway. I tried again on Monday. I pleaded with her. She said 'No' and looked quite alarmed. In the afternoon my form teacher sent for me and asked all kinds of snidey questions about Deborah. He obviously thought something disgusting – or at least deeply kinky – had been going on between us. I realised, too, that all my fuss might cause her hassle. And I didn't want anyone from school giving Deborah grief, no way. So I stopped trying to get her address and instead just prayed fervently that a teacher, and if possible Mrs Spacey, would be taken ill, and be replaced by Deborah, like before. And I was really convinced Deborah would come back.

But she never did. Months went by, teachers fell ill, new supply teachers turned up but never, ever her. She'd disappeared out of my life completely.

And then this evening I was hunting for something in my cupboard when I found the essay I'd written for her yonks ago. The one I should have handed in.

And I sat for ages thinking about her – the one woman – probably the only one – who was everything I'd ever wanted. And I could have made her happy. I know I could. But now it's too late. It's almost certain I'll never see her again. And I haven't even any pictures to remind me of her, nothing – except this essay.

It was then I realised the ending of my essay was wrong. And all at once I started rewriting. I was still frozen in the ice. But this time she suddenly plunged in beside me. Then the ice broke for a second time. But I managed to reach out and hold on to her as the ice reseated itself above our heads. The essay now ended like this: when they finally came to dig us out our death grip on each other was so strong they couldn't part us, and our bodies were eventually cremated together.

This new ending cheered me up no end. And I read and re-read it before finally returning it to the cupboard.

'Goodbye Deborah,' I whispered. 'Wherever you are.'

The Roseline Tape

Adèle Geras

One, two, three...testing, testing. Isn't that what you're supposed to say to a microphone? I don't know if this is the same, though. It's recording my voice, isn't it, and not amplifying it. I can't think why you need what you sometimes call 'my feelings' and other times call 'my version of events'. I mean, isn't this a loony bin? Isn't everyone here crazy, me included? Are the words of a loony to be trusted? I know you hate that word: crazy. You like words like 'disturbed' better, but I don't think I'm disturbed at all. It sounds messy, like a rumpled drawer. I feel quite tidy and well-arranged. In my own crazy way, of course. Are you catching all these words? I can see them as I'm speaking, squashing through the silver mesh at the front of this cassette recorder and coming out the other side as tape, all flat and shiny and brown. There they are, winding themselves round and round on to little black plastic spools. Have you ever seen a mincer? If you put meat in and turn the handle, red and white worms come out. If my words looked like that, all raw and bleeding, I wouldn't be a bit surprised, but it wouldn't half mess up your equipment, tee hee!

It's very quiet here. At the Roseline, it was very noisy. I find all this silence quite strange. You have to understand about the Roseline Hotel or nothing I'm going to tell you will make sense. Do you know the song 'Hotel California'? It's one of my best songs ever, about this hotel in the middle of a desert. In this song, it says that you can check out of the Hotel California any time you like but you can never leave it. The Roseline's just the same. It's with you always. It's with me now. The thing is, it's more than just an ordinary hotel. It's a kingdom. Huge. The biggest hotel on the Island, though not necessarily the best. We can accommodate five hundred people. We have bingo and cabarets every night. We have seven floors of bedrooms. We have the Barbados Bar, the Captain's Cabin Snuggery, the Writing Room, the TV Lounge, the Reception Area, the Poolside Bistro with the top bits of yellow beach umbrellas stuck to the yellow ceiling...how sunny and bright it looks even at 2 a.m! We have a dining room that stretches across acres of yellow carpet and in this dining room, waitresses in yellow dresses and white aprons flutter between the tables like small birds. My dad used to wear what he called his penguin suit and watch over the dining room: see that everyone had a table; arrange for this and that and the other to be done...he always told me it was a very responsible job, and I suppose it was. Tiring, too, at mealtimes, having to walk about like that, patrolling the strips of carpet between the tables, making sure everything was 'tickety-boo'. That was an expression my dad liked. 'Peachy-creamy' was another. Also 'hunky-dory'. He'd been to America once. His name was Arthur. He's dead now, but you know that, of course. It was an accident. That's what everyone says. But I'm not telling this in the right order. It's messy. You will have every right to call me disturbed if I carry on like this. Where was I? The Roseline...a kingdom. Yes.

Well, Molly is the Queen of the Roseline and she used to be married to the King of the Roseline, Howard. They had...they have...a son called Seth. Howard's brother, Roger, also works at the Roseline. He used to be in charge of the entertainments. Every evening at 8.00 in the Barbados Bar, under the whispering branches of the plastic palm trees, he'd call out the numbers for the bingo...clickety click...two fat ladies...Sherwood Forest...key to the door...and his silver-spangled jacket would glitter under the coloured lights, and all the guests would squeak and squirm with excitement. Seth and I used to laugh at him. Laugh at the guests, too, I'm afraid. They were always so shiny and pink from the beach: all the ladies so rustly and frothy in their new clothes bought specially for the holiday...and Roger used to flirt with them something rotten...touch them whenever he could, and make remarks about their figures and play stupid games with them on party nights where they had to pump up balloons hidden in the trousers of their gentlemen friends...oh, it was revolting. Roger was revolting. Woe betide any guest who was a bit overweight. He'd make fun of them non-stop. If it had been me, I'd have burst into tears, but the strange thing was, they loved it. They giggled and wriggled, and shrieked with laughter and all their separate chins and rolls of flesh shook and wobbled. Seth and I never stayed in the Barbados Bar for long.

'It's painful,' Seth used to say. '*He's* painful.' And he would shudder. 'How can two brothers be so different? I mean, look at him. Can you believe we're even related?'

That was Before. There's always a Before, isn't there, and an After? Before Howard died is what I mean.

I don't know if I can explain properly what everything was like Before. We were happy, all of us, that was the main thing. There was Howard, so tall and straight and dignified, running things. Managing whole battalions of maids, cooks, waitresses, cleaners, couriers, barmen and seeing to it that all the hundreds of visitors who came to

the Roseline all through the year, were happy. The
Roseline didn't have an out-of-season time. Not really.
We were open all the year round. That's like the Hotel
California as well. Any time of year, the song says, plenty
of room at the Hotel California. At Christmas time,
instead of the young families with small kids and couples
pretending not to be middle-aged, we had the old people
from the Mainland looking for somewhere mild to spend
the winter. The Island is supposed to be ten degrees
warmer than the Mainland. Did you know that? At the
Roseline, of course, it's warm all the year round. There is
a yellowness about the warmth. It wraps itself around you
like blankets. Howard and Molly must have liked yellow
as a colour: the whole hotel is decorated in shades of
yellow and orange and mustard and brown, but what you
think when you walk into it is: YELLOW. Still, as I say,
everyone was happy. Howard managed. Molly looked
glamorous in Reception and pinning the menus up on the
notice-board each day. She's yellow too. Have you seen
her? Yellow hair, up in a French pleat, and golden skin
and gold chains and bracelets and a love of tight, shiny
dresses. 'To show off my assets,' she used to say to me,
winking down at the breasts that swelled like melons
under her slippery clothes. Of course you've met her. She
must have been the one who brought me here. She likes
me. I think she thinks that as I haven't got a mother, she's
a sort of substitute. She used to say: 'I wish I had a
daughter like you,' and then she'd sigh. 'Boys,' she said,
'can be so difficult. Look at my darling Seth,' she'd say
and push her eyebrows up as far as they'd go. And Seth
was her darling, there's no doubt about that at all. I
thought all the kissing and cheek-pinching that went on
was a bit much, to tell you the truth, but it flattered and

amused Molly when people round the Island mistook them for boyfriend and girlfriend. They used to stroll round the shops hand in hand, and whenever they had a meal at a restaurant, Molly used to feed him little bites from her plate...oh, they were very close. Very close indeed. Still, I never thought Seth would react in the strange way that he did...but I haven't got there yet, have I? I'm getting ahead of myself. Anyway, I was attached to my father, too, but there certainly wasn't anything flirtatious about our feelings towards one another. Looking back, I think I probably loved my father to protect him from the fact that no one else did, as far as I could make out. Derek, my brother, could hardly spend an hour in his company without showing some kind of irritation...grinding his teeth, or shredding the edge of a paper napkin. But I loved my dad. I wish I'd told him that more often, but it's too late now, of course.

Molly was the first to have some idea of me and Seth getting together. Carrying on the Roseline dynasty. She used to give me things. Bits of jewellery and scarves and half-empty bottles of perfume. She'd sit me down in front of her mirror and show me how to put on make-up and how to twist my scarves like this and like that...I hated that mirror. It had two wings, one on each side, and when you looked into it you could see hundreds of different views of yourself, all sorts of unexpected images. I felt 'disturbed' in front of that mirror, I can tell you, as if I'd been broken into lots and lots of tiny splinters and would never get back together again. And none of it helped either. I'd watch what Molly did to my face with blusher and lip gloss, but when I tried to do it, later in my own room, I looked like a freak from a funfair, and I'd run to the bathroom and wash it all off. Looking at me, Molly would sigh sometimes and shake her head. 'Colour, lovey,' she'd say, 'that's what life is all about...colour. You're such a pale, quiet little thing...' and her voice would trail off into silence. I knew what she meant, though. She meant: how would I ever get a man, without all the colour and shine that men seemed to like? More particularly, how would I ever catch Seth's eye? It was a question I had been asking myself ever since I could remember. You have to understand something, little recording machine, something very important. I have loved Seth all my life. That's not so strange, is it? It's quite predictable. We grew up together. He is two years older than me. He is my own brother's best friend. We have roamed the corridors of the Roseline Hotel together since we were toddlers stealing sugar-lumps from the breakfast tables before the guests came down. No one did anything to discourage our friendship. Why should they? OK, he was the boss's son and I was only the dining room supervisor's daughter, but no one seemed to mind. Anyway, for years and years everything was fine. And then my brother Derek and Seth and I grew up. I noticed that Derek and Seth, during the summer holidays, seemed to be spending more and more hours at the edge of the swimming pool.

I have avoided mentioning the swimming pool for all this time – have you noticed? Is that significant, do you think? The swimming pool is the glory of the Roseline. It's irregularly-shaped, like two adjoining circles pushed out of true. There's a pale yellow paved area around it. There are deck chairs, and white tables with huge, yellow and white striped beach umbrellas stuck into their centres. Then there's a high wall round the pool, with climbing plants growing all over it...rambling roses, and wisteria and jasmine. There are also stone tubs dotted about here and there with flowers growing in them. At the edge of the pool there's an ice-cream and soft drinks kiosk. I have worked in this kiosk every summer since I was thirteen, and that's how it came about that I had such a good view of what Derek and Seth were doing. My dad called it 'cavorting'. This 'cavorting' involved a lot of laughter with young girls in bikinis; a lot of rubbing in of suntan lotion on backs and thighs and stomachs (let's see how near we can get to a breast, snigger, snigger); a lot of pretend-fighting and splashing in the water that allowed them to try and catch hold of the oily bodies, and that sometimes resulted in a bikini-top coming adrift...then there would be shrieks of pretend-horror, and little plump breasts like apples would bob about in the blue, and hands would touch them accidentally-on-purpose, and then the shrieking would start again, and then the girls would struggle out of the pool, all glistening like seals, and Seth and Derek would help to dry them off in yellow, fluffy Roseline hotel towels, and then the oiling would begin again.

'Frolicking'...that was another word my dad used. Also 'gambolling'. I just put scoop after scoop of pastel ice-cream into yellow wafer cones and felt as though my heart was being shredded. Do you know the way Kleenex tears raggedly and softly when you pull at it? That's what I felt like as I looked at Seth. Torn and soft and ready to crumple myself up and throw myself away. But I smiled at the children and doled out the ice-cream and no one ever knew. Not Molly. Not Derek, and certainly not Seth. Oh, no. Seth thought we were just as we'd been from the day we were born: good mates. We still had long chats together, we still giggled together at Ropey Roger doing

Adèle Geras

the bingo whenever Seth managed to tear himself away
from the pool and the lure of all that soft, greased flesh
turning golden in the sun. But we weren't the same. Not a
bit the same. Something had changed, and that was me. I
was different. I didn't look different. I was still thin, and
dark and pale, and I'd given up hope of ever having
breasts like melons, but I was different inside. And
because I was different inside, I wanted Seth to be
different in the way he treated me. There was one special
day when I noticed this. I'd always been jealous watching
Seth and Derek enjoying themselves at the pool, because
I wanted them not to forget my existence. I wanted to be
included in the general fun and games...the 'larks' my
dad called them. Anyway, on this particular day, I was just
taking some money from a little kid, and as I gave her
back the change, I saw that Seth and one of the oily girls
were far away from all the laughing, splashing others,
right down in the shallow end with all the babies,
practically under my nose. As I watched, I saw Seth push a
curtain of hair away from this girl's face, and I saw his
mouth being swallowed by her mouth, and then I saw
their bodies stretched out in the shallow water...stuck
together, and I felt as if my insides had turned to ice. I ran
out of the kiosk and into the loo and then I was sick. I
wasn't sick because I was disgusted. I was sick, I realized
afterwards as I sat in the loo, shaking with cold and pain,
because *I* wanted that: I wanted Seth's mouth fastened on
to my mouth, and his body pressed against mine, and his
hands rubbing fragrant oils into my skin. I was weak, sick
with wanting it. That was when I knew that my love for
Seth was different: different from what it had always been
and different from anything I would ever feel for anyone
else ever again. I could have asked to be moved from the

kiosk. I could have gone and looked after the babies in the crèche, and I wouldn't have needed to look at him, but I couldn't help it. I needed to see him, whatever he was doing. I wanted to look at the blue water and the deckchairs and the flowers growing up the wall. Sometimes Seth and the oily girl weren't there. I knew where they were. Once I had such a strong image of what they must be doing that I dropped four full double-choc cornets on the floor and burst into tears. Molly came and took me into her private sitting room and gave me a cup of tea. I pretended I was having my period, and she gave me some pills.

The thing about the oily girls was, they left after a couple of weeks. This one must have been special, though, because when she left, Seth went into one of his sulks. He often went into sulks. He stopped cavorting and frolicking and took to reading on his bed for hours without saying a word. I used to go in and sit with him sometimes.

'It's my A levels next year,' he said, when I asked him why he was doing so much reading. 'And then I'm off.'

'Off?' I said.

'To the Mainland. To university.'

I must have looked as sad as I felt, because he said, 'It's not the end of the world, you know. There's still the holidays.'

'But how will I live if you're not here?' I asked, and something in my voice must have struck him strangely, because he put his book down and looked at me. Looked right into me. He has these very pale grey eyes that seem to look inside a person…do you know what I mean?

'Won't you be happy?' he asked.

'I'll die.'

'Don't die. I'd hate it if you died.'

'Why?'

'What do you mean, why?' he asked. 'Because... because...'

'You can't say it,' I said. 'I can say it. It's easy. Look at me saying it. I love you.' I sat down on his bed, near his feet. He sat up at once and giggled. Then he said:

'And I love you too. There you are. I've said it.'

'But you don't mean it. You have to mean it.'

'I *do* mean it. I can't think of anyone except my mum and dad that I love better than you.'

'I don't mean like that.'

'Like what?'

'Like a sister or something.'

'What *do* you mean then?' He'd sat up by now. He started stroking his finger along the underside of my arm, very gently. I thought: my skin will blister and burn where he's touched it.

'I mean,' I stammered, 'I saw you. In the pool. Kissing that girl.'

'And what did you feel?'

I turned my head away so that he shouldn't see me. The words didn't seem to be able to get past my throat. Seth said again: 'What did you feel?' Only by now, his mouth was near my ear, he was whispering into my ear, so that I could feel his breath. 'Did you want it to be you that I was kissing? Yes? Did you?'

Oh, his breathing, his breathing and his voice blowing through my hair! I was becoming a volcano. I turned to him, and my mouth found his mouth, and although I'd never kissed anyone in my life before, I suddenly knew exactly how to do it, and all the feelings I'd had and all the love I'd felt came rushing out of me, covering me and Seth with white fire.

Much later, hours later, we went down to the pool to swim. We didn't cavort, or frolic or gambol, but we held hands and floated together in the turquoise water, and when our bodies drifted near one another, our swollen mouths would meet in a kiss that tasted of chlorine. When we got out, Seth wrapped me in a fluffy yellow towel, as if I were a baby. That was last year in September. September 6th, to be precise. I wrote it in my diary. I could show it to you. It says: 'Seth loves me. He said so.' He did say it. That afternoon and many times after that. He says now he didn't, but he did. He's so different now. I wrote it down, you see, so that there should be no mistake. But I can see that you might be a bit doubtful. I'm here, aren't I? On the funny farm...isn't it a bit suspicious that I can remember every word of a conversation like that? Didn't it sound a bit like a play I'd made up and memorised? I don't care, little machine. I don't care what you think, because *I* know. I know.

We were a couple after that. A pair. Everyone knew it. Molly remarked that I'd found a better complexion-improver than blusher, and giggled. She can be a bit crude, sometimes. Ropey Roger made jokes about us in the Barbados Bar. 'The young Prince of the Roseline and his lovely Princess,' he'd croon into the mike, and all the ladies' hearts would flutter looking at Seth. I was happy. He was mine for nearly a year, and then he went to university on the Mainland, and the whole world looked as though someone had switched the light off. That was Before. Then Howard died. Food poisoning, they said. One day he was fine and the next day he was dead. The Roseline went into mourning for a month. Seth came to the funeral, and then had to go straight back.

'I'll see you at Christmas,' he said, holding both my

hands at the airport, saying goodbye. 'Everything will be better. You'll see.'

But everything wasn't better. It was worse. Molly married Roger less than eight weeks after Howard's death. Some gossips said she must have been carrying on with Roger even while Howard was alive, but she hadn't.

'I don't know,' she said to me once as she was getting made-up for Talent Night in the Barbados Bar, 'why everyone has to be so unkind. I'm just the sort of person who *needs* a husband. I'd be quite lost without one. *You* know what I mean.' And she winked at me in the glass, woman to woman. I didn't know what she meant. I still don't. The idea of anyone else at all in all the world touching me in the way Seth does...the way Seth did...makes me want to vomit. As for Roger, I can't even feel sick. The thought paralyses me.

When Seth came back at Christmas and found them married, he changed completely. If I say, he went mad, you'll think I'm exaggerating. I'm not. He stomped around the place, being sullen. Rude to guests. Rude to Roger, and cold, cold, cold to me.

I asked him straight out in the Barbados Bar one night. A band was playing, so we had to speak loudly to be heard. I said:

'What's the matter, Seth? Can't you tell me? Don't you love me any more? Don't you remember how we were?'

'No,' he said. 'We weren't ever anything. You're imagining it. All you bloody women,' he shouted at me and his eyes blazed, 'you're all the bloody same. All you care about is sex. That's all you're interested in. Sex, sex, sex! I don't care if I never touch another woman ever again.'

I left then, and went to my room. I felt as if I were in a

coffin and the lid had closed on top of me. I felt suffocated.

I tried at first to make all sorts of excuses for him. His father dying – that was sad. His mother marrying someone he hated…that was enough to make a person miserable. And maybe there *was* something (just a teeny, weeny something) *more* about his feelings towards Molly that made him start behaving like her lover, because that's what he did. I can remember feeling, as well as the rawness and pain of being rejected by Seth, little stings of jealousy that he should be so concerned about his mother, and have so little interest in me. I'll give him time, I thought. He'll be better once he gets over all that.

Then, the row happened. Molly had summoned him to her room, probably to tell him off for the way he was carrying on. I think he must have been drinking. That was why, the police said, he had failed to notice my father in the drive as he roared out of the Roseline in Molly's car. I imagine my father, hit by that weight of metal in the dark, and I see his body spiralling up into the night, and coming down slowly, from high, high up, but I know it wasn't like that. They said the impact pushed him to the side of the road, where he died of a heart attack. One of the barmen found him, hours later, lying in a bed of wallflowers. Oh, Dad, I can't bear to think of you lying there all alone! I can't bear to think of all the things you might have been thinking as the hours passed. I try to think of you not knowing anything about what happened, and that makes me feel a little better.

Afterwards, Molly said Seth'd screamed and shrieked at her. I heard her telling the police. 'As if he were jealous,' she said. 'Can you believe it? As if he were a lover of mine and not my son…as if he'd become my husband…oh, it was grotesque. He kept on and on about the photos. Made me look at a photo of Howard, then at one of Roger… "How could you?" That's what he kept saying… "How could you leave this for this?" And then he shouted at me. Said he thought I was too old for…well, you know…all that side of things. They're so arrogant, the young, that's the trouble. Think they know it all. Anyway, he stormed out of here saying he was never coming back and (tears here and gulps of anguish) you know the rest. Poor Arthur!'

I can't get used to my poor old dad being dead. OK, I know he was a bit pompous. I know he was a bit of a bore who used funny words and behaved as though seeing five hundred people in to dinner were the same as organising the Battle of Waterloo, but still. He was my dad. I don't know what Derek will say when he comes back. He took a job on the Mainland last year, but he'll come back now. Not just for Dad but for me. To see what's happened to me.

Nothing's happened to me, though. That's the point. People thought I'd been drinking that night, but I hadn't. Some said the grief had gone to my head. I don't remember much about it. I remember going to the pool and picking all the flowers I could find. I remember vaguely coming into the Barbados Bar and handing flowers to everyone…I know I gave some to Molly. And to other people. I suppose I must have looked drunk. I suppose that was why they came after me later. I can remember thinking this: how lovely to lie in the black water of the pool and float and drift and pretend that it's still summer. I thought: if I close my eyes, I can pretend that it's still summer. I thought: if I close my eyes, I can pretend that the water is blue. My whole head will fill up with blue and summer and warmth. It will fill me, this blue water, like love. I will be filled with love. Death never really occurred to me. I only wanted to close my eyes and for everything to be blue again.

Molly found me, I think. She brought me here. I have had a visit from Derek. He says Seth should be locked up. He (Seth) is spreading stories in the town about how Ropey Roger (only he's calling him Randy Roger now) was the one who put poison in Howard's food and killed him. Derek says Seth talks wildly all the time. Of course, he has never been to see me. He doesn't love me any more. If he ever did.

It's pretty here. Lovely gardens. There's a brook over there. I can just see it from the window. When I've finished this recording, I think I'll go for a walk and look at it. I can see a willow bending into the water…how pretty it is! Someone ought to have a picnic on the bank. An imaginary picnic, perhaps. I'll pretend Seth is with me. I'll pretend we've just been married and he's crowned my head with posies of flowers and put garlands of bright leaves around my neck. I'll pretend I'm wearing a long, silk dress the colour of tea roses, and I'll pretend Seth loves me. I'll be down there soon, soon, little machine. Watch out for me. I'll be so happy, you'll hear me singing. By the stream. Over there. Under the willow branches.

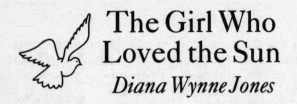

The Girl Who Loved the Sun

Diana Wynne Jones

There was a girl called Phega who became a tree. Stories from the ancient times when Phega lived would have it that when women turned into trees it was always under duress, because a god was pursuing them, but Phega turned into a tree voluntarily. She did it from the moment she entered her teens. It was not easy and it took a deal of practice, but she kept at it. She would go into the fields beyond the manor house where she lived and there she would put down roots, spread her arms and say, 'For you I shall spread out my arms.' Then she would become a tree.

She did this because she was in love with the sun. The people who looked after her when she was a child told her that the sun loved the trees above all other living things. Phega concluded that this must be so from the way most trees shed their leaves in winter when the sun was unable to attend to them very much. As Phega could not remember a time when the sun had not been more to her than mother, father or life itself, it followed that she had to become a tree.

At first she was not a very good tree. The trunk of her tended to bulge at hips and breast and was usually an improbable brown colour. The largest number of branches she could achieve was four or five at the most. These stood out at unconvincing angles and grew large pallid leaves in a variety of shapes. She strove with these defects valiantly, but for a long time it always seemed that when she got her trunk to look more natural, her branches

94

were fewer and more mis-shapen, and when she grew halfway decent branches, either her trunk relapsed or her leaves were too large or too yellow.

'Oh, sun,' she sighed, 'do help me to be more pleasing to you.' Yet it seemed unlikely that the sun was even attending to her. 'But he will!' Phega said and, driven by hope and yearning, she continued to stand in the field, striving to spread out more plausible branches. Whatever shape they were, she could still revel in the sun's impartial warmth on them and in the searching strength of her roots reaching into the earth. Whether the sun was attending or not, she knew the deep peace of a tree's long, wordless thoughts. The rain was pure delight to her, instead of the necessary evil it was to other people, and the dew was a marvel.

The following spring, to her delight, she achieved a reasonable shape, with a narrow, lissom trunk and a cloud of spread branches, not unlike a fruiting tree. 'Look at me, sun,' she said. 'Is this the kind of tree you like?'

The sun glanced down at her. She stood still as the instant between hope and despair. It seemed that he attended to the wordless words.

But the sun passed on beaming, not unkindly, to glance at the real apple trees that stood on the slope of the hill.

'I need to be different in some way,' Phega said to herself.

She became a girl again and studied the apple trees. She watched them put out big pale buds and saw how the sun drew those buds open to become leaves and white flowers. Choking with the hurt of rejection, she saw the sun dwelling lovingly on those flowers, which made her think at first that flowers were what she needed. Then she saw that the sun drew those flowers on, quite ruthlessly, until they died, and that what came after were green blobs that turned into apples.

'Now I know what I need,' she said.

It took a deal of hard work, but the following spring she was able to say, 'Look at me, sun. For you I shall hold out my arms budded with growing things,' and spread branches full of white blossom that she was prepared to force on into fruit.

This time, however, the sun's gaze fell on her only in the way it fell on all living things. She was very dejected. Her yearning for the sun to love her grew worse.

'I still need to be different in some way,' she said.

That year she studied the sun's ways and likings as she had never studied them before. In between she was a tree. Her yearning for the sun had grown so great that when she was in human form, it was as if she were less than half alive. Her parents and other human company were shadowy to her. Only when she was a tree with her arms spread to the sunlight did she feel she was truly in existence.

As that year took its course she noticed that the place the sun first touched unfailingly in the morning was the top of the hill beyond the apple trees. And it was the place where he lingered last at sunset. Phega saw this must be the place the sun loved best. So, though it was twice as far from the manor, Phega went daily to the top of that hill and took root there. This meant that she had an hour more of the sun's warm company to spread her boughs into, but the situation was not otherwise as good as the fields. The top of the hill was very dry. When she put down roots, the soil was thin and tasted peculiar. And there was always a wind up there. Phega found she grew bent over and rather stunted.

'But what more can I do?' she said to the sun. 'For you I shall spread out my arms, budded with growing things, and root within the ground you warm, accepting what that brings.'

The sun gave no sign of having heard, although he continued to linger on the top of the hill at the beginning and end of each day. Phega would walk home in the twilight considering how she might grow roots that were adapted to the thin soil and pondering ways and means to strengthen her trunk against the wind. She walked slightly bent over and her skin was pale and withered.

Up till now Phega's parents had indulged her and not interfered. Her mother said, 'She's very young.' Her father agreed and said, 'She'll get over this obsession with rooting herself in time.' But when they saw her looking pale and withered and walking with a stoop, they felt the time had come to intervene. They said to one another, 'She's old enough to marry now and she's ruining her looks.'

The next day they stopped Phega before she left the manor on her way to the hill. 'You must give up this pining and rooting,' her mother said to her. 'No girl ever found a husband by being out in all weathers like this.'

And her father said, 'I don't know what you're after with this tree nonsense. I mean, we can all see you're very good at it, but it hasn't got much bearing on the rest of life, has it? You're our only child, Phega. You have the future of the manor to consider. I want you married to the kind of man I can trust to look after the place when I'm gone. That's not the kind of man who's going to want to marry a tree.'

Phega burst into tears and fled away across the fields and up the hill.

'Oh, dear!' her father said guiltily. 'Did I go too far?'

'Not at all,' said her mother. 'I would have said it if you hadn't. We must start looking for a husband for her. Find the right man and this nonsense will slide out of her head the moment she claps eyes on him.'

It happened that Phega's father had to go away on business anyway. He agreed to extend his journey and look for a suitable husband for Phega while he was away. His wife gave him a good deal of advice on the subject, ending with a very strong directive not to tell any prospective suitor that Phega had this odd habit of becoming a tree – at least not until the young man was safely proved to be interested in marriage anyway. And as soon as her husband was away from the manor, she called two servants she could trust and told them to follow Phega and watch how she turned into a tree. 'For it must be a process we can put a stop to somehow,' she said, 'and if you can find out how we can stop her for good, so much the better.'

Phega, meanwhile, rooted herself breathlessly into the shallow soil at the top of the hill. 'Help me,' she called out to the sun. 'They're talking of marrying me and the only one I love is you!'

The sun pushed aside an intervening cloud and considered her with astonishment. 'Is this why you so continually turn into a tree?' he said.

Phega was too desperate to consider the wonder of actually, at last, talking to the sun. She said, 'All I do, I do in the remote, tiny hope of pleasing you and causing you to love me as I love you.'

'I had no idea,' said the sun and he added, not unkindly, 'but I do love everything according to its nature, and your nature is human. I might admire you for so skilfully becoming a tree, but that is, when all is said and done, only an imitation of a tree. It follows that I love you better as a human.' He beamed and was clearly about to pass on.

Phega threw herself down on the ground, half woman and half tree, and wept bitterly, thrashing her branches and rolling back and forth. 'But I love you,' she cried out. 'You are the light of the world and I love you. I *have* to be a tree because then I have no heart to ache for you, and even as a tree I ache at night because you aren't there. Tell me what I can do to make you love me.'

The sun paused. 'I do not understand your passion,' he said. 'I have no wish to hurt you, but this is the truth: I cannot love you as an imitation of a tree.'

A small hope came to Phega. She raised the branches of her head. 'Could you love me if I stopped pretending to be a tree?'

'Naturally,' said the sun, thinking this would appease her. 'I would love you according to your nature, human woman.'

'Then I make a bargain with you,' said Phega. 'I will stop pretending and you will love me.'

'If that is what you want,' said the sun and went on his way.

Phega shook her head free of branches and her feet from the ground and sat up, brooding, with her chin on her hands. That was how her mother's servants found her and watched her warily from among the apple trees. She sat there for hours. She had bargained with the sun as a person might bargain for their very life, out of the desperation of her love, and she needed to work out a plan to back her bargain with. It gave her slight shame that she was trying to trap such a being as the sun, but she knew that was not going to stop her. She was beyond shame.

'There is no point imitating something that already exists,' she said to herself, 'because that is pretending to be that thing. I will have to be some kind that is totally new.'

Phega came down from the hill and studied trees again. Because of the hope her bargain had given her, she studied in a new way, with passion and depth, all the time her father was away. She ranged far afield to the forests in the valleys beyond the manor, where she spent days among the trees, standing still as a tree, but in human shape – which puzzled her mother's servants exceedingly – listening to the creak of their growth and every rustle of every leaf, until she knew them as trees knew other trees and comprehended the abiding restless stillness of them. The entire shape of a tree against the sky became open to her and she came to know all their properties. Trees had power. Willows had pithy centres and grew fast; they caused sleep. Elder was pithy too; it could give powerful protection, but had a touchy nature and should be treated politely. But the oak and the ash, the giant trees that held their branches closest to the sun's love, had the greatest power of all. Oak was constancy and ash was change. Phega studied these two longest and most respectfully.

'I need the properties of both these,' she said.

She carried away branches of leafing twigs to study as she walked home, noting the join of twig to twig and the way the leaves were fastened on. Evergreens impressed her by the way they kept leaves for the sun even in winter, but she was soon sure they did it out of primitive parsimony. Oaks, on the other hand, had their leaves tightly knotted on by reason of their strength.

'I shall need the same kind of strength,' Phega said.

As autumn drew on, the fruiting trees preoccupied her, since it was clear that it was growth and fruition the sun seemed most to love. They all, she saw, partook of the natures of both oaks and elders, even hawthorn, rowan and hazel. Indeed many of them were related to the lowlier bushes and fruiting plants; but the giant trees that the sun most loved were more exclusive in their pedigrees.

'Then I shall be like the oak,' Phega said, 'but bear better fruit.'

Winter approached and trees were felled for firewood. Phega was there, where the foresters were working, anxiously inspecting the rings of the sawn trunk and interrogating the very sawdust. This mystified the servants who were following her. They asked the foresters if they had any idea what Phega was doing.

The foresters shook their heads and said, 'She is not quite sane, but we know she is very wise.'

The servants had to be content with this. At least after that they had an easier time, for Phega was mostly at home in the manor examining the texture of the logs for the fires. She studied the bark on the outside and then the longwise grains and the roundwise rings of the interior, and she came to an important conclusion: an animal stopped growing when it had attained a certain shape, but a tree did not.

'I see now,' she said, 'that I have by no means finished growing.' And she was very impatient because winter had put a stop to all growth, so that she had to wait for spring to study its nature.

In the middle of winter her father came home. He had found the perfect husband for Phega and was anxious to tell Phega and her mother all about the man. This man was a younger son of a powerful family, he said, and he had been a soldier for some years, during which time he had distinguished himself considerably and gained a name for sense and steadiness. Now he was looking for a wife to marry and settle down with. Though he was not rich, he was not poor either and he was on good terms with the wealthier members of his family. It was, said Phega's father, a most desirable match.

Phega barely listened to all this. She went away to look at the latest load of logs before her father had finished speaking. 'He may not ever come here,' she said to herself, 'and if he does, he will see I am not interested and go away again.'

'Did I say something wrong?' her father asked her mother. 'I had hoped to show her that the man has advantages that far outweigh the fact that he is not in his first youth.'

'No – it's just the way she is,' said Phega's mother. 'Have you invited the man here?'

'Yes, he is coming in the spring,' her father said. 'His name is Evor. Phega will like him.'

Phega's mother was not entirely too sure of this. She called the servants she had set to follow Phega to her privately and asked them what they had found out. 'Nothing,' the said. 'We think she has given up turning into a tree. She has never so much as put forth a root while we are watching her.'

'I hope you are right,' said Phega's mother. 'But I want you to go on watching her, even more carefully than before. It is now extremely important that we know how to stop her becoming a tree if she ever threatens to do so.'

The servants sighed, knowing they were in for another dull and difficult time. And they were not mistaken because, as soon as the first snowdrops appeared, Phega was out in the countryside studying the way things grew. As far as the servants were concerned, she would do nothing but sit or stand for hours watching a bud, or a tree, or a nest of mice or birds. As far as Phega was concerned, it was a long fascination as she divined how cells multiplied again and again and at length discovered that, while animals took food from solid things, plants took their main food from the sun himself. 'I think that may be the secret at last,' she said.

This puzzled the servants, but they reported it to Phega's mother all the same. Her answer was, 'I *thought* so. Be ready to bring her home the instant she shows a root or a shoot.'

The servants promised to do this, but Phega was not ready yet. She was busy watching the whole course of spring growth transform the forest. So it happened that Evor arrived to meet his prospective bride and Phega was not there. She had not even noticed that everyone in the manor was preparing a feast in Evor's honour. Her parents sent messengers to the forest to fetch her, while Evor first kicked his heels for several hours in the hall and finally, to their embarrassment, grew impatient and went out into the yard. There he wondered whether to order his horse and leave.

'I conclude from this delay,' he said to himself, 'that the girl is not willing – and one thing I do not want is a wife I have to force.' Nevertheless, he did not order his horse. Though Phega's parents had been at pains to keep from him any suggestion that Phega was not as other girls were, he had been unable to avoid hearing rumours on the way. For by this time Phega's fame was considerable. The first gossip he heard, when he was furthest away, was that his prospective bride was a witch. This he had taken for envious persons' way of describing wisdom and pressed on. As he came nearer, rumour had it that she was very wise, and he felt justified – though the latest rumour he had heard, when he was no more than ten miles from the manor, was that Phega was at least a trifle mad. But each rumour came accompanied by statements about Phega's appearance which were enough to make him tell himself that it was too late to turn back anyway. This kept him loitering in the yard. He wanted to set eyes on her himself.

He was still waiting when Phega arrived, walking in through the gate quickly but rather pensively. It was a grey day, with the sun hidden, and she was sad. 'But,' she told herself, 'I may as well see this suitor and tell him there was no point in his coming and get it over with.' She knew her parents were responsible and did not blame the man at all.

Evor looked at her as she came and knew that rumour had understated her looks. The time Phega had spent studying had improved her health and brought her from girl to young woman. She was beautiful. Evor saw that her hair was the colour of beer when you hold a glass of it to the light. She was wearing a dress of smooth silver-grey material which showed that her body under it when she moved was smooth-muscled and sturdy – and he liked sturdy women. Her overgarment was a curious light, bright green and floated away from her arms, revealing them to be very round and white. When he looked at her face, which was both round and long, he saw beauty there, but he also saw that she was very wise. Her eyes were grey. He saw a wildness there contained by the deep calm of long, long thought and a capacity to drink in knowledge. He was awed. He was lost.

Phega, for her part, tore her thoughts from many hours of standing longing among the great trees and saw a wiry man of slightly over middle height, who had a bold face with a keen stare to it. She saw he was not young. There was grey to his beard – which always grew more sparsely than he would have liked, though he had combed it carefully for the occasion – and some grey in his hair too. She noticed his hair particularly because he had come to the manor in light armour, to show his status as a soldier and a commander, but he was carrying his helmet politely in the crook of his arm. His intention was to show himself as a polished man of the world. But Phega saw him as iron-coloured all over. He made her think of an axe, except that he seemed to have such a lot of hair. She feared he was brutal.

Evor said, 'My lady!' and added as a very awkward afterthought, 'I came to marry you.' As soon as he had said this, it struck him as so wrong and presumptuous a thing to say to a woman like this one, that he hung his head and stared at her feet, which were bare and, though beautiful, stained green with the grass she had walked through. The sight gave him courage. He thought that those feet were human after all, so it followed that the rest of her was, and he looked up at her eyes again. 'What a thing to say!' he said.

He smiled in a flustered way. Phega saw that he was somewhat snaggle-toothed, not to speak of highly diffident in spite of his grey and military appearance, and possibly in awe of her. She could not see how he could be in awe of her, but his uneven teeth made him a person to her. Of a sudden, he was not just the man her parents had procured for her to marry, but another person like her, with feelings like Phega had herself. 'Good gods!' she thought, in considerable surprise. 'This is a person I could maybe love after all, if it were not for the sun.' And she told him politely that he was very welcome.

They went indoors together and presently sat down to the feast. There Evor got over his awe a little, enough to attempt to talk to Phega. And Phega, knowing he had feelings to be hurt, answered the questions he asked and asked things in return. The result was that before long, to the extreme delight of Phega's parents, they were talking of his time at war and of her knowledge, and laughing together as if they were friends – old friends. Evor's wonder and joy grew. Long before the feast was over, he knew he could never love any other woman now. The effect of Phega on him was like a physical tie, half glorious, half painful, that bound him to respond to every tiny movement of her hand and every flicker of her lashes.

Phega found – and her surprise increased – that she was comfortable with Evor. But however amicably they talked, it was still as if she was only half alive in the sun's absence – though it was an easy half life – and, as the evening wore on, she felt increasingly confined and trapped. At first she assumed that this feeling was simply due to her having spent so much of the past year out of doors. She was so used to having nothing but the sky with the sun in it over her head that she often did find the manor roof confining. But now it was like a cage over her head. And she realised that her growing liking for Evor was causing it.

'If I don't take care,' she said to herself, 'I shall forget the bargain I made with the sun and drift into this human contract. It is almost too late already. I must act at once.'

Thinking this, she said her goodnights and went away

to sleep.

Evor remained, talking jubilantly with Phega's parents. 'When I first saw her,' he said, 'I thought things were hopeless. But now I think I have a chance. I think she likes me.'

Phega's father agreed, but Phega's mother said, 'I'm sure she *likes* you all right, but – I caught a look in her eye – this may not be enough to make her marry you.'

Saying this, Phega's mother touched on something Evor had sensed and feared himself. His jubilation turned ashy – indeed he felt as if the whole world had been taken by drought: there was no moisture or virtue in it anywhere from pole to pole. 'What more can I do?' he said, low and slow.

'Let me tell you something,' said Phega's mother.

'Yes,' Phega's father broke in eagerly. 'Our daughter has a strange habit of –'

'She is,' Phega's mother interrupted swiftly, 'under an enchantment which we are helpless to break. Only a man who truly loves her can break it.'

Hope rose in Evor, as violent as Phega's hope when she bargained with the sun. 'Tell me what to do,' he said.

Phega's mother considered all the reports her servants had brought her. So far as she knew, Phega had never once turned into a tree all the time her father was away. It was possible she had lost the art. This meant that, with luck, Evor need never know the exact nature of her daughter's eccentricity. 'Sometime soon,' she said, 'probably at dawn, my daughter will be compelled by the enchantment to leave the manor. She will go to the forest or the hill. She may be compelled to murmur words to herself. You must follow her when she goes and, as soon as you see her standing still, you must take her in your arms and kiss her. In this way you will break the spell and she will become your faithful wife ever after.' And, Phega's mother told herself, this was very likely what would happen. 'For,' she thought, 'as soon as he kisses her, my daughter will discover that there are certain pleasures to be had from behaving naturally. Then we can all be comfortable again.'

'I shall do exactly what you say,' said Evor, and he was so uplifted with hope and gratitude that his face was nearly handsome.

All that night he kept watch. He could not have slept anyway. Love roared in his ears and longing choked him. He went over and over the things Phega had said and each individual beauty of her face and body as she said these things, and when, in the dawn, he saw her stealing through the hall to the door, there was a moment when he could not move. She was even more lovely than he remembered.

Phega softly unbarred the door and crossed the yard to unbar the gate. Evor pulled himself together and followed. They walked out across the fields in the white time before sunrise, Phega pacing very upright, with her eyes on the sky where the sun would appear, and Evor stealing after. He softly took off his armour piece by piece as he followed her and laid it down carefully in case it should clatter and alarm her.

Up the hill Phega went where she stood like one entranced, watching the gold rim of the sun come up. And such was Evor's awe that he loitered a little in the apple trees, admiring her as she stood.

'Now,' Phega said, 'I have come to fulfil my bargain, Sun, since I fear this is the last time I shall truly want to.' What she did then, she had given much thought to. It was not the way she had been accustomed to turn into a tree before. It was far more thorough. First she put down careful roots, driving each of her toes downwards and outwards and then forcing them into a network of fleshy cables to make the most of the thin soil at the top of the hill. 'Here,' she said, 'I root within the soil you warm.'

Evor saw the ground rise and writhe and low branches grow from her insteps to bury themselves also. 'Oh, no!' he cried out. 'Your feet were beautiful as they were!' And he began to climb the hill towards her.

Phega frowned, concentrating on the intricacy of feathery rootlets. 'But they were not the way I wanted them,' she said and she wondered vaguely why he was there. But by then she was putting forth her greatest effort, which left her little attention to spare. Slowly, once her roots were established, she began to coat them with bark before insects could damage them. At the same time, she set to work on her trunk, growing swiftly, grain by growing grain. 'Increased by yearly rings,' she murmured.

As Evor advanced, he saw her body elongate, coating itself with matte pewter-coloured bark as it grew, until he could barely pick out the outline of limbs and muscles inside it. It was like watching a death. 'Don't!' he said. 'Why are you *doing* this? You were lovely before!'

'I was like all human women,' Phega answered, resting before her next great effort. 'But when I am finished I shall be a wholly new kind of tree.' Having said that, she turned her attention to the next stage, which she was expecting to enjoy. Now she stretched up her arms, and the hair of her head, yearning into the warmth of the climbing sun, and made it all into limblike boughs which she coated like the rest of her, carefully, with dark silver bark. 'For you I shall hold out my arms,' she said.

Evor saw her, tree-shaped and twice as tall as himself, and cried out, 'Stop!' He was afraid to touch her in this condition. He knelt at her roots in despair.

'I can't stop now,' Phega told him gently. She was gathering herself for her final effort and her mind was on that, though the tears she heard breaking his voice did trouble her a little. She put that trouble out of her head. This was the difficult part. She had already elongated every large artery of her body, to pass through her roots and up her trunk and into her boughs. Now she concentrated on lifting her veins, and every nerve with them, without disturbing the rest, out to the ends of her branches, out and up, up and out, into a mass of living twigs, fine-growing and close as her own hair. It was impossible. It hurt – she had not thought it would hurt so much – but she was lifting, tearing her veins, thrusting her nerve ends with them, first into the innumerable fine twigs, then into further particles to make long sharp buds.

Evor looked up as he crouched and saw the great tree surging and thrashing above him. He was appalled at the effort. In the face of this gigantic undertaking he knew he was lost and forgotten and, besides, it was presumptuous to interfere with such willing agony. He saw her strive and strive again to force those sharp buds open. 'If you must be a tree,' he shouted above the din of her lashing branches, 'take me with you somehow, at least!'

'Why should you want that?' Phega asked with wooden lips that had not yet quite closed, just where her main boughs parted.

Evor at last dared to clasp the trunk with its vestigial limbs showing. He shed tears on the grey bark. 'Because I love you. I want to be with you.'

Trying to see him forced her buds to unfurl, because

that was where her senses now were. They spread with myriad shrill agonies, like teeth cutting, and she thought it had killed her, even while she was forcing further nerves and veins to the undersides of all her pale viridian leaves. When it was done, she was all alive and raw in the small hairs on the undersides of those leaves and in the symmetrical ribs of vein on the shiny upper sides, but she could sense Evor crouching at her roots now. She was grateful to him for forcing her to the necessary pain. Her agony responded to his. He was a friend. He had talked of love, and she understood that. She retained just enough of the strength it had taken to change to alter him too to some extent, though not enough to bring him beyond the animal kingdom. The last of her strength was reserved for putting forth small pear-shaped fruit covered with wiry hairs, each containing four triangular nuts. Then, before the wooden gap that was her mouth had entirely closed, she murmured, 'Budding with growing things.'

She rested for a while, letting the sun harden her leaves to a dark shiny green and ripen her fruit a little. Then she cried wordlessly to the sun, 'Look! Remember our bargain. I am an entirely new kind of tree – as strong as an oak, but I bear fruit that everything can eat. Love me. Love me now!' Proudly she shed some of her three-cornered nuts on to the hilltop.

'I see you,' said the sun. 'This is a lovely tree, but I am not sure what you expect me to do with you.'

'Love me!' she cried.

'I do,' said the sun. 'There is no change in me. The only difference is that I now feed you more directly than I feed that animal at your feet. It is the way I feed all trees. There is nothing else I can do.'

Phega knew the sun was right and that her bargain had

been her own illusion. It was very bitter to her; but she had made a change that was too radical to undo now and, besides, she was discovering that trees do not feel things very urgently. She settled back for a long low-key sort of contentment, rustling her leaves about to make the best of the sun's heat on them. It was like a sigh.

After a while, a certain activity among her roots aroused a mild arboreal curiosity in her. With senses that were rapidly atrophying, she perceived a middle-sized iron-grey animal with a sparse bristly coat which was diligently applying its long snout to the task of eating her three-cornered nuts. The animal was decidedly snaggle-toothed. It was lean and had a sharp corner to the centre of its back, as if that was all that remained of a wiry man's military bearing. It seemed to sense her attention, for it began to rub itself affectionately against her grey trunk – which still showed vestiges of rounded legs within it.

Ah well, thought the tree, and considerately let fall another shower of beech mast for it.

That was long ago. They say that Phega still stands on the hill. She is one of the beech trees that stand on the hill that always holds the last rays of the sun, but so many of the trees in that wood are so old that there is no way to tell which one she is. All the trees show vestiges of limbs in their trunks and all are given at times to inexplicable thrashings in their boughs, as if in memory of the agony of Phega's transformation. In the autumn their leaves turn the colour of Phega's hair and often fall only in spring, as though they cling harder than most leaves in honour of the sun.

There is nothing to eat their nuts now. The wild boar vanished from there centuries ago, though the name stayed. The maps usually call the place Boar's Hill.

The Authors

Annie Dalton is the author of *Out of the Ordinary* (Methuen) and *Night Maze* (Methuen). She writes: 'Asked for a love story I panicked until I remembered the camel bag my father bought in Alexandria. Then I realised I could write about a girl paralysed with fear that family history will repeat itself, as confused about herself and 'love' as I had been, yet who learns, like Molly in *Out of the Ordinary*, and Harriet in *Night Maze*, that if we trust the selves we are, dreams, fears, warts and all, we can allow the transforming power of love to flow through us without needing to either protect ourselves from it, or abandon ourselves in its name. And then maybe we really could heal the world.'

Ian Strachan's most recent novel, *The Flawed Glass* (Methuen) was shortlisted for the 1989 Whitbread Award. He writes: 'I survived life in the entertainment industry in the sixties and seventies without abusing drugs – one or two of my friends didn't and some of them aren't around any more. I believe there are better ways to face up to pressure and, like Pete in 'Crack Down', I would rather experience all the pleasure and pain of life with my senses intact. Just as Peter did when he turned his back on his parents in my book *Moses Beech*, or Lee when his family left Vietnam to face typhoons and pirates on their *Journey of a Thousand Miles* and Shona, the severely disabled heroine of *The Flawed Glass*, who retains her sense of magic and wonder in the face of tremendous physical problems.'

Jenny Koralek writes: 'I found it one of the most difficult things I've been asked to do – to try and write about love and, in this case, the heartache it can cause. The words of the 60s song kept coming back to me: 'What's it all about, Alfie?'

'For me it means being able to be yourself, your true self with the other person and letting them be able to be their true self, so that you are both alone – that is all-one, yet not lonely. Body and soul together. One or the other by itself will never last or fully satisfy. Heartache is always about loss. But on the flipside, and there always is a flipside, heartache stops our capacity to feel from shrivelling like a nut left over from last Christmas, or from turning into a heavy stone. True love, true sorrow can make us less careless about others and look in a new way at every face one sees.'

'Sea Changes' is Jenny Koralek's first story for teenagers.

Geraldine Kaye writes: 'I lived in both Asia and Africa for some years and many of my books such as *Comfort Herself* and *A Breath of Fresh Air* reflect this experience. 'The Key' is about another kind of conflict, the difference between home and school or school and another school. The main character, Holly, has to deal with the upheaval in her life imposed by her father's redundancy and the more private but equally overwhelming upheaval of an uncertain first love.'

Jean Ure writes: 'In common with most compulsive writers, I can't remember a time when I haven't wanted "to be a writer". I wrote my first novel when I was six. It was about a little girl called Carol who went off to collect her friends for a party. The novel went on for two and a half pages of a scrapbook and was a long list of all my favourite names – Carlotta, Bianca, Natasha, Patricia … (No boys' names: at six years old I was instinctively sexist.)

I wrote a great many novels before I had my first one published. They were all written in exercise books stolen from the school stationery cupboard and were all, without exception, derivative. When I was fourteen I wrote a wish-fulfilment book called *Dance For Two* (which was also derivative), and this was published while I was still at school.

But if writing was the major passion of my teenage years, love certainly ran it a close second. At various times, from the age of eleven, I was in love with: the school cricket captain (a strapping girl most unfortunately named Mary Bigg and jovially referred to by my father as Bigg Mary); Fred Trueman (I was very into cricket); Sir Malcolm Sargent; Dirk Bogarde; Antonio (this was during my Spanish dance period) and a French singer called Gérard Souzay, who was the Great Love of my Life until I went to drama school and fell in love with my husband, with whom I have remained in love ever since.'

Jean Ure's most recent novels published by Methuen are *Plague 99*, *After Thursday* and *Tomorrow is Also a Day*.

Pete Johnson writes: 'I've always hated those "Love is" cartoons and especially their terminally cute captions, "Love is holding your partner's hand even when she's just sneezed on to it."

'Yet, all my stories are love stories perhaps because I've never sussed love out – and writing is also an incredible form of investigation.

'Before I wrote *Catch You on the Flip Side* I and my notebook went back to teenage parties and saw again, just how tense asking a girl out can be. I can stand anything but rejection. That's why in *The Cool Boffin* I picked a character whom everyone likes but no one wants to go out with. While in *I'd Rather be Famous* I looked at two main characters who had been going out together for a year and were becoming a little careless of each other.

'Just how powerful is Love? Can it survive even death? That's the question at the centre of my ghost story *We the Haunted*. I'd like to think that nothing good every really goes away. It's there – a part of us, forever.'

Pete Johnson's most recent novel is *I'd Rather Be Famous* (Methuen).

Adèle Geras writes: 'Love, sitting in the centre of a cobweb of allied interesting emotions, is very enjoyable to write about, and the torments of love (which are dreadful if you're going through them yourself) are best of all. I try, if I can, to make my readers feel what the characters are experiencing, even if they have to suffer at one remove. Fiction is a great consolation, although it doesn't prepare us for our own real pain. The pleasures of love are harder to describe, but they more than make up for all the anguish, which is why we keep falling in love over and over again. The real problems start when (as in my story) you think that love is once only, and forever.'

Adèle Geras has written two collections of love stories: *The Green Behind the Door* and *Daydreams on Video*.

Diana Wynne Jones writes: 'I do not regard myself as good at writing love stories. Our two sexes strike me as so different that it surprises me that they ever get together at all. Perhaps for this reason, when I do write about love, I nearly always have to have one of the lovers in some guise which is not their own, as I did in *Howl's Moving Castle* and *Dogsbody*. But having written *Fire and Hemlock* about human lovers for once, I thought I might manage that kind of story for *Heartache*. Not a bit of it. The story refused to come until one of my sons and one of my sisters were both, for different reasons, studying Ovid's *Metamorphoses*. Thinking about what they were doing, I felt that Ovid had got things slightly wrong: all his people get changed into something else by gods. But surely, I thought, if people are going to change, they do it for themselves. Hence the story.'

Diana Wynne Jones's most recent novels are *The Lives of Christopher Chant* and *Wild Robert*.

TAKE YOUR KNEE OFF MY HEART

Edited by Miriam Hodgson

'Love demands songs, really.'
David Johnstone

'We usually make complete idiots of ourselves when we fall in love.'
Mary Hooper

'Love has a way of reaching into every corner of our daily lives.'
Marjorie Darke

Nine superb new love stories to make you laugh and cry, including stories by Marjorie Darke, Mary Hooper, Monica Hughes, Pete Johnson, David Johnstone, Anthony Masters, Jenny Nimmo, Ann Pilling and Dyan Sheldon.

THE TEENS BOOK OF LOVE STORIES

Edited by Miriam Hodgson

'When one is first afflicted by the pangs of love,' writes K. M. Peyton, 'the symptoms are not treated with much sympathy by the older generation. "Calf-love" they call it, and laugh.'

In this specially commissioned collection of stories, love is portrayed in *all* its many guises with realism and humour . . .

With contributions from Vivien Alcock, Berlie Doherty, Mollie Hunter, Anthony Masters, Michael A. Pearson, Joan Phipson and Alison Prince.

A Selected List of Fiction Available from Mandarin

While every effort is made to keep prices low, it is sometimes necessary to increase prices at short notice. Mandarin Paperbacks reserves the right to show new retail prices on covers which may differ from those previously advertised in the text or elsewhere.

The prices shown below were correct at the time of going to press.

☐	7493 0003 5	**Mirage**	James Follett	£3.99
☐	7493 0134 1	**To Kill a Mockingbird**	Harper Lee	£2.99
☐	7493 0076 0	**The Crystal Contract**	Julian Rathbone	£3.99
☐	7493 0145 7	**Talking Oscars**	Simon Williams	£3.50
☐	7493 0118 X	**The Wire**	Nik Gowing	£3.99
☐	7493 0121 X	**Under Cover of Daylight**	James Hall	£3.50
☐	7493 0020 5	**Pratt of the Argus**	David Nobbs	£3.99
☐	7493 0097 3	**Second from Last in the Sack Race**	David Nobbs	£3.50

All these books are available at your bookshop or newsagent, or can be ordered direct from the publisher. Just tick the titles you want and fill in the form below.

Mandarin Paperbacks, Cash Sales Department, PO Box 11, Falmouth, Cornwall TR10 9EN.

Please send cheque or postal order, no currency, for purchase price quoted and allow the following for postage and packing:

UK   80p for the first book, 20p for each additional book ordered to a maximum charge of £2.00.

BFPO   80p for the first book, 20p for each additional book.

Overseas   £1.50 for the first book, £1.00 for the second and 30p for each additional book
including Eire   thereafter.

NAME (Block letters) ....

ADDRESS ....

....

....